D0374513

IN SHADOWS WE FALL

DEVIN MADSON

978-0-9954133-4-4 (pbk)

Edited by Amanda J Spedding
Cover art by John Anthony Di Giovanni
Cover Design by STK Design

For all the heroes history forgot.

The Imperial Expanse of Kisia

WINTER 1355

Creeping is a stupid thing to do if you don't want to be seen. Wearing black is equally suspicious. The greatest asset of any assassin isn't the ability to go unseen, it is the ability to be seen and yet go unremarked.

I strode along the passage, through pools of darkness and onto their lit shores. Most of the light came from the hearts of intricately carved lanterns hanging overhead like suns, but nearing the corner diffuse light glowed through a screen door. A soft laugh. Footsteps. I walked on wondering who Lady Zin was entertaining tonight. As she got older her men only seemed to get younger.

My wooden sandals snapped upon the wooden floor, but though I cared little for stealth my heartbeat snapped with them. It had sped to a panic the moment I left my room and there it stayed, turning my stomach sick.

It has to be done. It has to be done.

Despite the late hour a servant bustled toward me, a tray balanced on one hand. They stopped. Bowed. Scurried on. I tried not to hurry, though the thud of my rapid pulse urged speed.

It has to be done.

The door came into sight, a flicker dancing upon its paper panes. Still awake, but there was nothing for it. I could only hope he was alone as I had not come prepared to slit the throats of two.

The felt runner hushed the slide of the door. Inside a lamp flickered low, its light touching the dark hair of a man kneeling at the table. His head had slumped forward onto his arm and for a tense moment I thought him already dead, but he snuffled and ground his teeth and slept on.

The door slid silently closed.

A lump moved upon the sleeping mat, more snuffling proving the existence of the fair company I had dreaded. Perhaps now stealth would not be such a terrible plan. If the woman was smart and slept on then she would not have to die.

No wooden boards here, but my steps caused the reed matting to crackle – no more than the crackle of a fire, but enough to disturb a light sleeper. Step. Pause. Nothing. My fingers found the worn leather of the knife hilt in my sash. Step. Pause. The man dozed on. He had been writing, the half finished letter caught under a bent arm.

Not a moment too soon.

My knife failed to glint dramatically in the light, but it did not fail to pierce the soft skin of the man's neck. His throat offered resistance like aged meat, but I had no time for finesse. I ripped the blade through it, spraying blood. His eyes opened. He wheezed. Bubbled. Failed. Crimson spilled upon the page before I could snatch it away, though snatch it away I did. Just as wide, fearful eyes found me they began to roll back, though whether he recognised my face I would never know.

A flailing arm caught the lantern sending it tumbling onto the matting. No crash of broken glass, but the flame flickered and died as its owner did, a last sigh heralding the beginning of his next journey – judgement.

Movement sounded from the mat. "Irash?"

With no time to stow the dripping blade, I darted for the door, heart in my throat. But as I touched the wooden frame light flared, basking the room in a tender golden glow. A young woman sat upon the mat, her hair in some semblance of a Lady's Knot though she was no lady. A yiji brought in for the entertainment of an important guest, perhaps, although it didn't matter. Her quick fingers had doomed her.

"Empress Li!" the woman dropped the flint box and flattened herself into a bow upon the fine silk coverlet. "Your Imperial Majesty, I am but your humble servant."

"Then I am very sorry," I said, walking toward the sleeping mat. I had not wanted anyone else to die. But it needed to be done and discovery – even suspicion – would be the end. The emperor was not a forgiving man.

"Sorry?" The girl sat back up and her eyes darted to the dead man for the first time, the sight paling her face despite its thick paint. "Y-Your Majesty, please, I will never tell a soul, I swear. Please let me go."

I knelt beside her and she flinched, but did not run. Servants did not run from an empress.

"Please, you cannot do this to me," she said, lifting her hands in supplication. "Please!"

"I can," I said. "And I must. Because I know what he will do to me if he finds out."

She rasped her last breaths as the man had done, blood gushing down her neck to stain her nightrobe. Her eyes widened too, hands clinging to me as every gurgled gasp became more of a struggle. I wanted to push her away and run, to let her die where I did not have to see, but I could not. This, I told myself, holding her gaze while the last of her life drained away, is what he has brought me to. But this is nothing to the ruin that is coming.

Numb, unsteady steps took me back to my apartments, the girl's blood smeared upon the crimson silk of my robe. I had once heard that crimson was the imperial colour so that imperial soldiers could hide their injuries in battle. Whether it was true or not I was grateful for it now. Grateful, too, that the inner palace appeared to be asleep. I passed no one in the passages, saw no living creature until I came to my own rooms where two Imperial Guards stood sentry.

"Your Majesty," they said. Neither so much as glanced at my bloodstained hands. Nor did they bow. It was not wise for a soldier on duty to let down his guard, even in the demonstration of proper respect.

"Koto. Cheng." I nodded to each in turn. "I heard some very odd noises while I was taking my nightly walk and I am afraid there might be intruders. Do check my rooms to be sure no one is lying in wait."

Nods. "Yes, Your Majesty."

Though wisdom dictated that one should remain outside on guard, they both entered, Koto in front and Cheng closing the door behind. My apartments were warm and inviting after the chill horror of the emissary's room. A woven carpet covered part of the matting floor and an army of braziers warmed the air. Painted screens

4

and decorative vases of dried flowers spoke much of Kisia's culture, but whatever lies history tried to spin for the people it would not keep enemies at bay. Neither would their gods.

"It is done then?" Koto said, his eyes hard beneath slanting brows.

"It is done," I said. "Unfortunately he had a woman with him."

"Dead?"

"Yes."

"Good."

The man paced across the floor with heavy booted steps. "It should buy us time."

"The only question is how much time." Cheng folded his arms and leaned against the doorframe. "I don't like how fast this is moving."

"For all we know he could have been planning this even before the treaty was signed," I said, clenching and unclenching my hands as the blood dried.

Cheng grunted, the lines of his aging face wrinkling in disgust. "Exactly the sort of thing he would do. He is not going to be pleased about this."

"That's why we did it," Koto said.

"Why *I* did it," I interrupted. "Do not forget whose hands are stained." I held out my bloody fingers for emphasis. "Do not forget who is risking everything."

Koto bowed then. "We do not forget, Majesty, but we are in this mess together now."

"Mess is right," Cheng muttered from the doorway. "I ought to have retired already and be well out of it. Ought to have gone back to the farm."

"But you did not, dear friend," I said.

"More fool me!"

For a moment there was no sound above the hiss and click of the braziers. In the outer palace the business of ruling Kisia never stopped, and beyond its walls the city of Mei'lian never slept, but here in the very heart of the empire there was only silence.

"And the oligarch?" Cheng again, not having moved from the doorway. He had been the most reluctant conspirator, yet there was no one I trusted more.

"I'm working on it," Koto said, the harsh lines of his face deepening to ferocity. "I have gained access to an informant inside his household. It's not going to be easy, but if we can't get to him then we'll have to involve the ministers."

Cheng grimaced. "A dangerous road."

Though Koto snorted I had to agree. The Minister of the Left and the Minister of the Right were the Emperor's chief advisors, the ones he relied upon above all others. But they were also men who would not take kindly to being kept in the dark, or to finding out the emperor was making deals with pirates and barbarians behind their backs.

"Scoff all you want, Captain," Cheng said. "I'm a simple man, always have been and hope I always will be, but I've been here more years than you've been able to—" a glance at me. "...shave. And I can tell you that making the truth known might well quash the emperor's plans, but if it doesn't lead to a coup or a war with his brother then you can call me a bear's—" another glance my way, this time accompanied with a wry grin. "...grandmother."

"I think we are on informal enough terms now to dispense with such niceties," I said. "If we have to involve the ministers and no war follows, I'll be quite happy to call you a bear's cock, Cheng, though it might lead to some interesting questions."

The man chuckled, the same warm, friendly chuckle I had first heard back in Chiltae. Cheng had been one of the company sent to escort me south with a handful of court ladies. They had been stiff and haughty and had looked down their noses at me, and when Cheng had caught me sticking my tongue out at them behind their backs he had laughed. Of such small moments are friendships built.

"*That*," Koto said, bringing the conversation back on track. "Is why we are trying it your way first. If the Chiltaens can apply pressure on the ministers and the ministers apply that pressure to the emperor, then there is a chance we can get through this without anyone needing to know anything about it. Then we can go our separate ways and never speak of this again."

Cheng nodded. "And I can retire to that farm."

"If that is what you want," Koto returned with a shrug.

"When you get to be my age it's what you'll want too. Trust me, Captain."

"I doubt that."

Before Koto could do more than sneer, I said: "And General Kin? Do we have to worry about him?"

Koto turned his disdain from Cheng's farm to the absent general. "He'll ask questions, he always does, but the fool hasn't yet figured out that his steward likes to gossip. He's good, but not good enough, and soon the emperor will realise that."

"And put you in his place?" Cheng said. "If being the leader of Emperor Lan's guard is your ambition then this is the last place you ought to be."

"Being the leader of the Imperial Guard is my ambition," Koto said. "But I never said anything about Emperor Lan." His gaze flicked my way. He knew I had no love for the emperor, but even Koto knew doubt. And if he wanted to serve as General of the Imperial Guard under Emperor Lan's heir, then he would need my blessing. Prince Yarri was old enough to make most of his own decisions, but not so old his mother could not whisper in his ear.

"Those are dangerous words." Cheng folded his arms. "I'm going to pretend I didn't hear them. Stopping this foolish alliance if we can is one thing. Assassinating the..." He stopped. "We ought to go back to our posts before General Kin gets wind that we wandered off."

Once they had gone I stood alone in the centre of the floor and let out a long breath. The blood had dried upon my hands, tightening the skin, but though Zuzue had left a bowl of water I did not move. I had killed before, had walked these halls and sent men to their final judgement before they could have me sent to mine, but this was different. This was the first time I had killed for something bigger than myself. For Kisia. And the first time I had killed a woman.

But it had to be done. When it was my turn to face the gods I could only hope they would judge me with that in mind.

A SEER ONCE TOLD ME I WOULD DIE BEFORE MY THIRTIETH year. I watched the soldiers tie her to the stake. "I don't believe in fate," I said, though I could not meet her gaze.

"You don't need to," she returned, those her last words

before flames engulfed her, charring her skin and hair and bubbling her fat. "Fate believes in you."

Most nights she returned in my dreams, but it was never the scream that woke me. It was never the peeling of the seer's skin or the moment when her flesh broke, leaking fat, that saw me wake covered in a sweaty tangle of sheets. The Emperor had laughed when the burning body – long silent – had dried and twisted, lifting its limbs into crooked positions like a wooden puppet. I had told him it was disrespectful to laugh at the dead, and that was the moment I always woke, the moment he turned to me and laughed again. "She wouldn't be dead at all if not for you, my dear."

I woke with those words once more ringing in my ears and my skin damp beneath my night robe. Light shone in around the edges of the shutters, while the tink of hot coals in the brazier was further proof it was long past dawn. Despite the braziers the cold bit at my face and I rolled, snuggling into the womb of warmth the feather duvet afforded.

Parchment crackled beneath my pillow. A small scroll bound in string had been wedged beneath it, flattened by the weight of my head. Only Zuzue could have put it there without waking me, able to bring a blanket of silence to everything she did. It was a handy trait in a maid but even more important in a messenger.

Unrolled, the scroll bore only a few words in blocky, clumsy characters.

You know where. Trouble.

There is nothing quite like a vague message of danger

to send one's heart racing. I rose from my mat into the biting air. Even the matting upon the floor seemed to crackle like ice. The note shrivelled safely away to nothing when dropped upon the coals, but barely had it vanished before the door slid upon its hushed felt feet, and in the opening Zuzue bowed. "Your Majesty," she said.

"It was Cheng?"

She did not look at me. It was not allowed, no matter how long she had been in my service. "Yes, Your Majesty."

"Then you must help me dress. Quickly."

"Yes, Your Majesty."

A warm woollen under robe had already been laid out along with its silk companion, and it was with well-practiced hands that she shook first one then the other and held them up. I stood and let her dress me, all the while staring at the glowing coals. A bed of coals had been placed beneath the seer before she burned, the executioner concerned that the chill damp of winter would make it difficult to keep heat upon such a soft, fat old woman. He had wanted it to be spectacular, to serve as a warning, and it had worked. The emperor had commended him personally.

"Anything?" I asked.

"Nothing official," she said. "But Little Torono, one of the under maids, has been removed from her work and no one has seen her since dawn. There are plenty of whispers. Most seem to think she has been caught with child, but one of the kitchen boys swears he saw a dead body being carried down under a sheet."

"Do they say who?"

"No, Your Majesty. The boy was whipped."

Her words ought to have settled the worst of my fears,

but the bubble in my gut only grew. Silence didn't mean safety. The emperor didn't want his court to know his unnamed guest had been a scion of the Curashi Tribe – barbarians whose relationship with Kisia could only be described as tense and bloody. In fact, those two words could describe the relationship between Kisia and every one of its neighbours. They were not good at making friends.

Zuzue tied a complex knot in my crimson sash, leaving the Otako pikes to swim down the tail that remained. I knelt then and let her attend to my hair, juggling pins and combs and a damp cloth to ease stray hairs into place. It always took a long time, longer because my hair was golden and harder to see, Zuzue said, but today it fretted me more than usual, the continued unrolling of time picking at my fears.

"How are the children?" I said, more to pass the time than because I expected news.

Fingers continued their dance across my scalp. "Juno said Prince Takehiko had a fitful night, but is well, Your Majesty. Also Princess Hana might be cutting her first tooth."

The little noise of maternal delight came easily enough, though my thoughts were far removed from the baby tucked in her crib with her nurse in attendance. Safe. Loved. I needed to ensure she stayed that way. War was not good for children.

"She says, too, that Prince Rikk is to be moved out of the nursery," Zuzue went on. "He is to join his brothers at their studies."

Surely it was not so long since he had been a baby in my arms, but in truth it was a lifetime ago. Before the emperor had stopped looking at me. Before my indiscretion. Before I had killed a man merely for what he had seen. Back when the treaty with Chiltae was a sought-after necessity and no plan of inviting barbarians and pirates to betray us had been in Emperor Lan's head.

Before the seer.

Again my gaze slid to the coals. The woman had screamed, but not for as long as I had expected. By the time her skin had peeled her cries for mercy had ceased – the voice of prophecy silenced.

"Finished, Your Majesty. I shall paint your face now."

I knew not how long it was before I escaped from Zuzue, unsatisfied with the face that looked back from the mirror. There was always a new line, or another stray hair to pluck, age seeming to have a cruel sense of humour.

The gallery was empty but for Cheng, yet I strode in as though with every intention of looking upon the portraits of the emperor's ancestors. Many wore the same great crimson robe he donned every day, and all looked down from their places with varying degrees of haughty disdain. Their expressions chilled my bones as surely as did the cold air and I hugged my fur stole about my shoulders.

"Your Majesty," Cheng said, the snap of my sandals drawing his attention. There seemed to be more lines upon a face already criss-crossed by life. "You're alone?"

"As you see. Only Zuzue knows I have risen from my mat. She says he is repressing talk, so what is the trouble?"

Cheng looked toward the window, beyond which the snow-dusted gardens blocked much of the outer palace from view. "The trouble is that the alliance was signed this morning."

"But I killed their emissary." The words were little

more than breath stolen from my lungs, but his grimace showed he caught them all the same.

"There must have been another or you killed the wrong man, I don't know, but I saw it signed with my own eyes."

"Koto?"

A bow for show, though he still did not meet my gaze when he rose. "He says you must see Lord Epontus tonight. Koto will organise everything. Only men he can trust."

"Tonight?" My heart beat like a tolling bell. "Then tell him I will take Prince Takehiko with me."

"Again? Are you sure, Your Majesty?"

"Yes, very sure. I cannot do this without him."

Cheng frowned, but though he had lent himself to this little mutiny, in truth he had been too long a soldier to argue with me. He had none of Koto's fire. None of Koto's ambition.

"I will tell him."

"Is there anything else?" I said. "I ought to join the court before my absence is remarked. If His Majesty has completed this alliance he will be in one of his... jovial moods."

The old soldier shifted his weight from one foot to the other. "Nothing else, Your Majesty, but I wouldn't go to the throne room today. A warning from an old friend."

I glanced around at the empty gallery because I could not meet his gaze. "She's there, isn't she?"

"Yes, Your Majesty. General Kin, too, who is out of favour with the emperor after last night's events. He is hunting the assassin and we do not want his eyes to turn to you."

"No. We don't." My fingers curled into fists. "That

would just give His Majesty a fine excuse for getting rid of me."

And the man who gave him that excuse would be richly rewarded. General Kin was the son of a soldier. Or perhaps a blacksmith. I ought to know. Of such small pieces of knowledge was power built.

I gazed unseeing upon the portraits for a time before making my way up the stairs to the fourth round of the inner palace. There the gathering court bustled. Heads turned, and as I strode into the antechamber bows spread through the crowd like grass bending before the wind, spreading murmurs of "Your Majesty" like a susurrus. It followed me to the great black doors of the throne room, both open so crimson light could spill out like blood. Coloured by the glass in the high windows, it blanketed all in a red-hued haze, making mockery of all the finely-painted faces.

Upon the grand lacquered throne the emperor sat at his ease, and though he did not often laugh he was laughing now, his eyes crinkling as he looked at the woman sitting on the divan beside him. My divan. She was a glorious young thing – that I could not deny – her skin a creamy hue and her hair so black it shone beneath the crown of a single jewelled comb. Jingyi had served me before she bled, when youth had protected her from most of the court's wandering eyes. But time had given her a fine figure and a pair of laughing eyes, along with the emperor's undivided attention.

As I approached she made a show of rising from the divan so I might take it, but under every watching eye the emperor bade her remain. Conversations trailed off. Eyes turned from them to me. Grateful for the paint upon my cheeks, I stiffened my back and strode to the Humble

14

Stone. There, in a clearing of silk trunks, I knelt to bow before Emperor Lan. Never had I wanted to do so less, never had I hated the laughter in his eyes so much I wanted to scoop them out. Such dreams calmed my fury as I knelt waiting, the time before he asked me to rise cruelly long.

"Long life, Your Majesty," I said as I rose, but he was not looking at me. This man who had called me his glorious sun, who had lain with me and fathered my children, at whose side I had sat through all the years of our marriage and he could not even spare me a glance. His attention was all upon Jingyi. Her bright red lips smiled a sensual promise.

Thus dismissed, I turned and found my eldest son watching from a distance. The heir to the crimson throne excused himself from his usual circle of hovering sycophants and came across the floor. "Mama," he said, something all too like a smirk twitching curved lips. "It looks like I was right after all."

"Poor form to rub it in my face at such a time, Yarri," I said, and though I drew myself up, at only thirteen he was already taller than me.

"Poor form for you to be so blind you don't see it coming. I used to think you knew everything. Did you know that Rikk is to come out of the nursery? It will be amusing to have another little brother to play tricks on. Tanaka has gotten too smart to fool."

While he spoke the prick of dozens of eyes touched my skin. Perhaps Cheng had been right and I ought not to have come, but any excuse would have declared defeat and those false smiles of pity would have become smiles of triumph. In all these years few members of the court had truly accepted me, and even my own son had

15

come to realise that being seen with me did him little good.

"Will you call her mother when I am gone?"

The question surprised a frown from him. "Lady Jingyi? I don't know. Should I?"

"Not unless you want me to rip her throat out."

He laughed. "You wouldn't."

It seemed a woman's purpose in life was to be underestimated. But I could hardly blame him. Yarri was his father's heir more than he was my son. Lan had seen to that, removing him from the nursery and from my influence early. He had learned to walk and talk the emperor he would one day become.

"Perhaps not," I said, taking a deep breath to cover the pain of realising I could not trust my own blood. "You ought not be seen speaking to me now it seems His Majesty's mind is made up."

"I thought of that, but it would also look very bad of me not to honour my mother with a few words." He bowed, tipping forward hair kept so short no one would see how much like mine it was. "Long life, Your Majesty."

"And to you, Your Highness."

I stayed in the throne room as long as I could bear it, avoiding the pull of my gaze toward the throne. But I could not keep myself from turning when the emperor laughed. A mischievous smile came with Jingyi's reply, the girl smiling as much for the court as for him with so many gazes upon her. That had been me once, and it was with bitter satisfaction that I told myself her star would not stay long aloft. In a few years another pretty girl would come along and Jingyi, too, would be thrown aside.

As I turned my gaze from the emperor's laugh-slitted eyes, it was General Kin who caught my attention. He stood beside the throne as he always did, but it wasn't the emperor he watched. Despite Cheng's warning the man had no reason to suspect me, yet for all the aloof unconcern I attempted my heart hammered all the same. Even now Koto would be organising a group of guards that could be trusted with silence, guards loyal to him and to me, not to General Kin.

That thought wriggled uneasily in my mind. Of such thoughts are rebellions built.

———

Darkness fell upon the palace. Soft treads passed my door, and in the distance gongs tolled the hour, their rich voices calling out to every secretary and servant – the army of brightly-coloured ants that kept Kisia alive while the emperor was busy smiling at Jingyi.

One of the treads stopped, but it was not Koto. A man entered, the crimson slash upon his shoulder proclaiming him one of the emperor's personal servants. He bowed, eyes averted, and said: "His Imperial Majesty will see you now."

Not a request – an order, no more amenable than the instructions he gave his lowest servants. I tried to still the rising panic with a long, slow breath, but dread spun on in my mind. How much did he suspect?

"Of course." I knew how to sound confident and proud, and I nodded to Zuzue as she cleared away the remnants of my dinner. No words were needed. She would warn Koto if I did not soon return.

It was too short a journey to require a procession, but I let the man lead the way, every watercolour scroll and screen like an old friend. From outside the emperor's apartments General Kin watched us approach. Perhaps one day someone would make him smile, but until then he was stiff and unyielding, always appearing older than his years ought to have allowed. But age hadn't been the only objection to his appointment. However impressive his reputation, Kin was no nobleman.

"Your Majesty," he said when I stopped before the doors. And though it was not required from an Imperial Guard on duty, he bowed. Deeply and with more grace than expected, leaving my haughty sniff sounding rude.

"His Imperial Majesty sent for me," I said.

"Yes, Your Majesty."

He slid one of the great doors and stepped in. "Empress Li is here, Your Majesty."

"Good. Good," spoke the emperor from inside, his voice owning no warmth. "Send her in."

General Kin stepped back, his crimson surcoat whispering as it touched my robe. He looked away. "You may enter, Your Majesty."

Though it was an overlarge room, the emperor's main apartment was unseasonably warm, braziers seeming to occupy every spare space. The hiss and click of their coals provided winter's music, overlaid with the soft crackle of the reed matting beneath my feet. Emperor Lan watched me enter. He lounged in a Chiltaen-style chair with his feet crossed in front of him, and not a word did he speak as I knelt to bow. Once again he left me there much longer than was necessary.

"You may rise, my wife," he said at last. "If you can with such creaky bones."

I got to my feet with every ounce of grace and ease I could muster. "I am not yet so old as that, Your Majesty," I said, biting off the observation that he was older than I by sixteen years.

He grunted like a frustrated hog. There had been a time when I had found him handsome, when his smile had lightened the harsh lines of his features, when an earnest desire to rule well had given him dignity, but those days had passed. He had changed. Kisia, too. Perhaps the war had changed more than I had seen, safe in my fine palace.

"I was pleased to receive your summons, Your Majesty," I said, the measure of truth in the words bitter on my tongue. It had been a long time.

"Of course you were. And I am loath to disappoint you but this will be a short meeting." He shifted in his chair and leaned forward, his bright eyes upon me. "Things are about to change, Li. I am going to return Kisia to its glory. I am going to conquer the northern heathens and when I do, it cannot be with an aging Chiltaen empress at my side, her figure soft and her hair paling. No, when Chiltae are once again our vassals I must have another empress, one who represents everything that makes Kisia great. No more treaties. No more negotiations. No more merchant commoners nibbling away at our border and eroding our history and our culture. We are the oldest. The greatest. The wisest. And we will prevail as the gods have always intended."

"But our treaty—"

"To the hells with treaties, did you not hear a word I said?"

I had, every rousing word washing over me with greater horror. "Yes, I did, Your Majesty," I said, and looking him in the eye I began to lie. "But I don't think I understand. Has something changed? Were we not losing the war before the treaty was signed?"

Go on, I urged. *Crow about your clever plans. Tell me how you've just signed a secret contract with the Curashi. Tell me about the hundreds of fully-manned ships you're getting from Lord Eastern, the Pirate of Lin'ya, in return for nothing but your niece's maidenhead. Tell me about your plans to raid the Ribbon, to destroy the Chiltaen fleet, to set fire to their dockyards and crush any who try to resist. Tell me so I can tell you how all that will end.*

"Kisia does not lose wars."

It was hard not to laugh. Chiltaen history told a different story. "Of course not," I said. "When one has gods on one's side one does not tend to lose wars."

"Finally come to your senses then, have you?" he said. "Given up on your foolish Chiltaen god?"

"I have lived in Kisia longer than I lived in Chiltae, Your Majesty."

Another of his grunts. "Then you will accept their decree and go quietly."

"The gods themselves wish me gone?" I should have known he would take the easy road, that he would steal away all chance to fight. Who could argue with the gods?

His sage nod stirred the bile in my gut. "They have spoken to me, yes," he said. "And success hangs upon your departure."

"Did the seer tell you so?"

I saw the same leer in my dreams, when over and over again the woman burned. "You want to know what she told me? She told me that Kisia would be one land, from the Ribbon to the south sea, and that it would be ruled by the descendants of my blood, its glory everlasting."

And she had told me I would die. That my children would die. That the empire would burn. Doubt gnawed at my mind. Perhaps it was not the war I had to fear. Perhaps it was only this man, this arrogant, hateful man who would put another in my place because my figure had grown soft with the bearing of children, because my hair was the wrong colour and my heritage no longer useful. Descendants of his blood did not have to be descendants of mine. Jingyi could already be carrying a new heir.

You will die before your thirtieth year.

I balled my hands to keep them from trembling. "Then of course I will go," I said, thoughts tangling as I tried to clutch at something, anything, that could make him change his mind. As soon as I was out of sight how easy it would be to be rid of me and my tainted children.

A thought struck me like summer lightning, as frightening as it was stunning. It began to unfold before me, each thread leading to another, only to be interrupted by the emperor's voice. "Something you want to say, Li?"

His eyebrows were raised in a weary sort of interest. There was so much I wanted to say, so much I had kept to myself year after year because to speak ill of the emperor was treason. To disagree with the emperor was treason. To even look askance at the emperor was treason. When I didn't immediately answer he lifted his brows higher still. "Well?"

"I was only thinking..." I let the words hang, hating myself for them but knowing nothing else would so surely put him off the scent of growing treason in my mind.

"Thinking what?" he prompted.

"That we might lie together one last time before I leave."

He laughed, that same mocking laugh that haunted my dreams, but he beckoned me closer and I went, the treason in my heart giving me a fierce joy such as I had never known.

"WELL?" KOTO SAID, POUNCING ON ME THE MOMENT I returned to my room.

"He knows nothing. At least if he knows something he isn't saying so, but he did admit he plans to invade Chiltae."

A snort, not even the pretence of respect. "Unless we can strip away his new allies. Did he say anything else?"

I shook my head, hair loosing from what was left of Zuzue's fine styling. To speak of my own dismissal would make it real, losing me not only my empire, my husband and my children, but Koto too. What ambitious captain would clutch at the skirt of a falling star?

"He was merely in the mood to boast," I said. "Call for Zuzue. She must fix my hair and fetch Takehiko before we go."

"Are you sure about the boy?"

"Yes."

"He just fell asleep last time."

"I'm sure, Koto. Do it."

He bowed then, recalling, too late to my mind, that I was still his empress.

IT WAS COLD IN THE PALANQUIN. MY BREATH FORMED A cloud and my fingers had turned to curls of ice. At the peak of a bad winter the streets of Mei'lian were choked with snow, but still I hurried the carriers on. They would be fortunate if their fingers did not grow so numb they dropped their poles.

The nest of furs upon my lap shifted and snuffled,

growing one fair cheek. The light of lanterns passing overhead lit the rest of the face in flashes – a mess of sandy hair, a small turned-up nose and lips made pink by the cold – all smushed against a clenched hand. He was asleep and I dared not move lest he wake. He was going to need all his energy tonight.

We soon left the lit streets behind and Prince Takehiko vanished into the night, only his weight upon my legs and his snuffling proving his existence. The palanquin turned. Slowed. Outside shouts and laughter proved that even the bitter cold could not completely halt a city about its business. Bright lights illuminated one curtain of the palanquin and the plaintive sound of a shamisen sang to the bare moon, but even that was soon gone and we plunged back into darkness. And in that darkness my new plan blossomed, the enormity of it both thrilling and frightening. I could not trust it to Koto. Not even to Cheng. Some roads had to be walked alone.

Boots crunched snow as the carriers stopped, bringing my attention back with a jolt. Whatever choice I made, I had to get through this meeting first.

"Takehiko." I shook the boy. "We are here."

He snuffled again and opened his eyes. "I'm sorry, Mama," he said, blinking rapidly and pushing himself up out of his nest. "I fell asleep."

"You are forgiven. But you must straighten yourself. We do not go before any eyes looking untidy."

"No, Mama."

I set a hand to my hair, checking pins and elaborate curls by touch. Robe. Sash. Sleeves. The fur stole around my shoulders. Eyes upon me, Takehiko ran through the same routine with a three-year-old's clumsiness. I adjusted the sit of his crimson sash for him, the knot so big and elaborate that it almost covered his whole torso.

"Good," I said when I was satisfied. "Off you go."

With one hand upon the curtain he hesitated, his little face twisting. "You are afraid, Mama."

"It is wise to be afraid, my child, but not wise to show that fear to others. We are Otakos. We show no fear."

"No, Mama." Still he hesitated. "The soldiers are afraid too."

"It is their job to fear everything so they can keep us safe. Now go, we cannot keep our host waiting too long or it will appear rude."

"Yes, Mama."

He pushed the curtain aside and climbed out onto the mounting block, met by murmurs in the chill air as every soldier bowed. A small smile hovered about my lips, only to be stolen a moment later by the fear he had felt, the fear I had tried to bury out of sight. Perhaps he was getting stronger. Or I weaker.

I stepped out after him, and he offered me his hand as though he had been the emperor himself. I took it, forcing a smile though his touch tingled like something at once both too hot and too cold.

Easier not to think about it.

The carriers had halted outside a discreet house in a narrow backstreet, exactly the sort of place one expected for such meetings. The single lantern above the door ought to have illuminated the steps and a portion of the road, but all its failing flame managed was the wooden door and the stern face of Koto. He bowed but did not speak. It was not necessary. The warning he would have uttered stood clear upon his furrowed brow.

Despite the spluttering lantern we were expected, and

the door opened as I set my foot upon the step. No face appeared. No light. Just a maw that opened into darkness. A mother's instinct was to enter first, but protocol maintained power. Let one slide and the other would follow.

Without glancing back, Takehiko went first up the stairs. Even at three the protocol had been so firmly drummed into his head no amount of fear could shift it. Suffused with pride, I followed.

Inside, a servant bowed, traces of moonlight dancing about his short white hair. "His Lordship apologises for the darkness. It is merely a precaution. Do follow me."

The door shut with a click leaving only a dim light calling us along the passage. Not bright enough to see clearly, but it guided our way, sandals crunching fresh reed matting. The light sat beyond the paper screens of a highly carved door and there the servant stopped to bow before sliding it open.

A round table took up most of the room beyond. Paintings and carvings hung upon the walls, but it was the shape of the table more than any ornamentation that flaunted Chiltaen wealth. Such a waste of wood – rosewood too, if my eye was not out.

The man sitting at the table rose, letting furs fall to reveal a sumptuous silk robe in shades of green like a dappled forest floor. Not an old fashioned robe, but one in the new style, no doubt made especially for him. No interest in tradition then, a fact worth remembering.

"Your Highness," he said, bowing to Takehiko. The boy did not find this very interesting. His gaze had slipped toward another door set behind a steaming brazier.

The man bowed again to me. "Your Imperial Majesty. I am greatly honoured by your visit."

"A visit I trust will remain between us."

Again he rose, this time with an amused smile. "Indeed it shall, but what a loss to my business to have a visit from the Kisian Imperial family kept secret."

"You mistake," I said. "Were it known, then your business would be in very grave trouble indeed."

"Opening with a threat, Your Majesty?"

"A warning, My Lord Oligarch."

"Epontus, please," he said. "As no one will ever know about this meeting we may as well be informal, don't you think?" His eyes slid to Takehiko, whose sleepy gaze moved about the room from picture to carving to coloured glass ornament. "You bring a child to protect your honour, Your Majesty?"

I had practiced my smile until I could form it perfectly at need, and did so now. "I protect my own honour, Lord Epontus. The presence of my son is merely the whim of a devoted mother."

Again his eyes slid to the boy and I wondered what he had heard. Whispers travelled. Even, it seemed, when mouths had been silenced.

The smile that spread his broad lips was as practiced as my own and he indicated the table already set with tea and sweets. "Do join me, Your Highness. Your Majesty."

Takehiko brought his attention back to the man and one of his brows twitched. But he said nothing, just ran his small hands down the front of his robe before kneeling. Those small hands grabbed a fur blanket from the floor and pulled it around him, forming something like the nest he had made in the palanquin. It was not the action of a prince, but the sooner the man forgot his presence the better, so I just placed a hand upon the boy's head and patted his hair, cooing like a mother dove.

I let the clink of ceramic and the clearing of the lord's

throat draw me out of my motherly pretence. "Tea, Your Majesty?"

A nod. Empresses didn't say thank you.

Lord Epontus shifted his portly bulk, leaning an elbow upon the table to better reach the steaming pot. A drawback to having a fancy round table.

Tea splashed as he poured, and though I pretended not to notice, he gestured to the servant kneeling by the door. The man rose and mopped up the spilt tea, but when he ought to have returned to his place he lingered. It was the man with the white hair who had let us in, but despite the colour he was not old. He risked a glance my way. Such disrespect could earn him the lash. I ought to have objected, but the danger of my own position stilled my lips and all too soon the moment passed.

Protocol maintains power. Let one slide and the other will follow.

"Leave us, Gadjo."

The servant bowed, murmured and departed, all while Lord Epontus, with some effort required to move his bulk, set the steaming tea bowl before me. He then gathered up his own as though his hands were cold, but then perhaps he was. In Chiltae it hardly ever snowed and the Ribbon never froze.

"Foul stuff," Lord Epontus said, taking a sip and shuddering. "I never will understand why you Kisians prefer tea over wine."

You Kisians. I had spent half my life in Kisia. Was that what it took to be disowned? Or was I no longer useful?

"They drink wine," I said. "Just not as frequently as we Chiltaens imbibe it. It is served after meals. Warmed in the winter."

If he noted my attempt to regain my heritage he didn't

show it. "Madness," he said. "But there is never any accounting for foreign ways. Did you know that across the Eye Sea there's a land that has no ruler? They are nomads – horsemen – who follow their herd leader and no one else. One would think they would fight often, but people say the grasslands are so immense that they don't fight because they have everything they need. Fascinating, eh?"

"Very." I took a sip as Takehiko snuggled against my thigh. "But I did not come to talk about horsemen from across the sea."

"Of course not, Your Majesty. So do enlighten me."

He seemed to have forgotten about Takehiko, probably thought the boy asleep though I knew he wasn't. He never could sleep with strangers close by, their souls pressing in upon him.

"The treaty," I said. "You signed it."

Eyebrows went up. "I did. As did the other oligarchs. Also your husband, the Great Emperor of Kisia, may he live forever, and his brother Grace Tianto. In fact it was signed by everyone of importance."

I forced out my smile, though would have loved to choke the words 'everyone of importance' from his throat.

"Peace, you see," he went on. "Is good for trade."

"Yes," I said. "And for people not dying."

"Trade is also good for people not dying, if it is life you care about, Your Majesty. Though I would point out, with no malice intended, that it was Kisia that invaded us this time."

"This time."

His laugh shook his bulk. "I am sure you are aware, Your Majesty, that we have, shall we say, a... colourful history?"

"I am aware. But you seem to be unaware that your peace is in jeopardy."

Lord Epontus set his bowl down with a thud. "Ah, now I was wondering what all the secrecy was about. You've heard something? You wish to be of service to your people at last?"

"I have," I said, ignoring the last jab. "If one lives long enough at the Kisian Court one grows long ears. The details are my own to keep, but if you want the peace to last then you must organise a marriage between one of your merchant lords and Lady Kimiko Otako."

"Grace Tianto's daughter? She is the Emperor's niece!"

"Yes."

"Why?"

"Because if you do not then trade won't be good for quite some time."

"That is all? You expect me to petition for a marriage on such tenuous grounds? You'll excuse me for being frank, Your Majesty, but there is a reason why you Kisians have been happy to take Chiltaen brides but we do not take Kisian brides. They are too expensive. The offer the family would have to make to Grace Tianto would be so immense as to not be worth it. War would be preferable!"

"And if I could see to it that the price was... considerably lower?"

He scoffed. "Oh yes, only half crippling. Even so I would be hard pressed to find a family acceptable to the Otakos that would be willing to pay such a price merely for a woman. Too proud by half," he went on, his colour rising. "The Otakos think their fancy throne makes them gods, well their people may believe such rot but we are not so blind. Men are men. We built Chiltae on that belief and are proud of it. No one would give a fortune for the girl be she never so pretty, because the Otako name means nothing on the Ribbon."

He must have realised to whom he was speaking for he puffed out his cheeks and bowed an apology. "I let my tongue run away with me, Your Majesty. But in all truth, I could find you a dozen rich families happy to sell their daughters to the Otakos, hells even a few who would pay some small amount for the honour, but not the other way around."

And water the Kisian blood further. There had been enough trouble when I had married Emperor Lan, or Prince Lan as he had been then. And there had only been more bloodshed since. No, that would not work. It had to be Lady Kimiko.

I sipped my tea. It had gone tepid but still calmed fraying nerves. Cheng would be disappointed, Koto not surprised, but I had done what I could. Now all I needed was to be sure of the man's silence.

Beneath the table my fingers wriggled into Takehiko's hair. The boy held his breath.

"It is unfortunate that we were unable to come to an understanding," I said, setting down the half-empty tea bowl. "You will of course speak not a word of this meeting or its contents to anyone."

"Of course, Your Majesty," Lord Epontus said. "Not a word, on my honour. You are in enough trouble at court I think, without adding to it."

My hand stilled amid Takehiko's curls. "Trouble?"

The man laughed. "I am sure I can find a new husband for you, Your Majesty. Even the Otakos would not expect much for old goods. I hear the Emperor's latest is quite something."

"Men have their appetites," I said, lifting my chin.

"Women too." His glance shied to the still form of Takehiko curled at my side. "At least so I hear."

My free hand balled into a fist, but I sent my practiced smile in to battle. "Indeed. Your word on your silence?"

Lord Epontus bowed as low as he could before the table got in the way of his stomach. "My word."

"He's lying."

The muffled words came from the furs, but Takehiko didn't lift his head.

"Excuse me?" the Lord Oligarch said. "Did he—?"

"*His Imperial Highness* does not think you are telling the truth, yes," I said. "But he is just a child, of course, children take such whims into their heads, especially to protect their mothers. Do allow me to apologise on his behalf, Lord Epontus."

Lord Epontus grunted. "Yes, well, he ought to learn to keep his mouth shut."

"Indeed he should." With one hand still upon Takehiko's head, my other crept to the thick band of my sash where wriggling fingers soon found steel. The knife came free and, heart thumping hard now, I tucked it behind my back and made a show of rousing the sleepy prince.

"We have trespassed upon His Lordship's fine hospitality too long, my son," I said. "It is time to leave."

I rose with the words. The Lord Oligarch would have to rise too, and bow, for that was the custom and however much he might detest Kisia respect had to be paid. He struggled a little to gain his feet, but once there executed a proper bow, sliding his hands down the front of his fine silk robe. "Your Highness. Your Majesty," he said. "It has truly been an hon—"

My slash cut the flesh of his neck, missing his throat but spilling hot blood onto my hand. He buckled, his bulk

31

crashing a knee into the matting. I lashed out again to finish the job, but he moved and the blade juddered into his cheekbone only to leap from my hand like a slippery fish.

Lord Epontus hissed, a hand pressed to his neck where the slash bled. He might still die if he bled out. "Damn you, woman!" he snarled, his other hand steadying himself upon the table. "If you want me dead then do it properly. Order your guards to do it so at least it'll be clean."

He got his bulk to its feet, teeth clenched hard. "Gadjo!" he said. "Gadjo!"

"Master?" the word came as the door slid, no amount of silent prayer managing to keep it closed. I froze, blood smearing my hands.

The silver-haired servant took in the room with a sweeping glance. From his master, barely standing, to the tousled boy at the table, to me, then down at the blood-drenched dagger upon the reeds.

"Run for the surgeon, man!" Lord Epontus snapped, his face growing pale. "Her Majesty is leaving."

Gadjo bowed. "Your Lordship."

Almost I called him back, my hand twitching toward him as though to grasp his collar as he turned, but in the space of a breath he was gone taking my secret with him.

"You can be sure the rest of the oligarchs will find this as interesting as your previous request, Your Majesty," Lord Epontus said, struggling for breath. He leaned against a decorative sideboard. "But if you do not wish the emperor to hear of it then I suggest you go now."

An offer made to the foolish woman he thought me.

The dagger lay a step away, maybe two in this tight robe. Lord Epontus was in no fit state to fight and the longer I waited the weaker he became, but there might be more servants or even guards he could summon with a scream.

A breathy laugh interrupted my thoughts. "Is it really so desperate, Your Majesty, that you would kill me for my silence? You are Chiltaen. You ought to be on our side."

You will die before your thirtieth year. Your children will die. The empire will fall.

The clear certainty of the seer's gaze troubled me though her eyes had long been burned away.

"I refuse to die," I said and reached for the dagger. My fingers closed around it before he could move or speak and I thrust as I turned. His hand caught my wrist. The grip not strong, but it twisted, sending sharp pain through my arm until the dagger fell again. But he did not let go, instead yanked me close, smothering me in the stink of blood.

"For this I will make sure you die," he snarled, lips drawn back to reveal well-kept teeth. "Attacking an oligarch is an attack on the treaty, which is treason against your Emperor. He's been after an excuse to replace you with fresher meat and now he can have it."

I cried out as he twisted my arm as though trying to snap the bone. Tears sprang to my eyes. "No, you cannot," I said. "Let me go! I am—"

"Do not hurt Mama," came the small voice from the table. "I am a Prince of Kisia and I command you to let her go."

Lord Epontus did, slumping back, shaking, against the sideboard. "Of course, Your Highness," he said with a dry laugh. "My apologies. Now how about you take your Mama and get out of my house. I would not want her death on my hands."

I fell to my knees, tears blurring the room. The foolish tears of a woman tired of having to fight, of having to smile, to pretend, to do whatever was requested of me. Tears at having failed Koto and Cheng, at having failed Kisia, at having failed to keep the interest of the Emperor long enough that I might have been spared the humiliation that was to come.

The oligarch's voice came in a huff. "What are you doing?"

Takehiko had risen from his place at the table, leaving behind his cosy nest of furs to approach the bleeding man. "I am leaving," the boy said. "But before I go you must bow to me. It is the law."

Another dry laugh, but although he did not kneel, Lord Epontus bent forward. As his head reached the lowest point injury and fat would allow, Takehiko gripped the man's blood-streaked cheeks between his small hands – hands that had not yet shed the plumpness of youth.

"What—?"

"I am doing what my mother wants," the boy said, pulling the oligarch's head down when the man tried to stand. "I have to protect her. She is afraid."

"I can—" the word ascended into a scream, the sound there and gone as it rose to a pitch his voice could not reach. The scream went on in silence, his eyes popping from his head as every breath came fast and shallow.

The whole scene lasted mere seconds. From touch to scream to the moment the oligarch crumpled to the floor like an enormous baby birthed from between its mother's legs. And there, curled tight, he remained. Still. Not a sound. Not a breath. Nothing.

Takehiko's eyelids drooped, the eyes behind them

seeming to glaze in fatigue. "Can we go home now, Mama?" he said. "I want Juno."

"Yes, of course," I said, my heartbeat seeming to have taken over from the oligarch's, racing in its place. I wanted to ask what he had done but feared the answer. The boy ignored the man curled upon the floor, not so much as glancing at him when I scrambled to retrieve my blood-stained dagger.

I am doing what my mother wants, he had said.

I held out my blood-stained hand for his, closing it upon his slick little fingers though I wanted to pull away. Only the crackling of the brazier sounded in the room. It might have been best to hide my tea bowl so it appeared the oligarch had been alone, but Gadjo knew better and would be back any moment with the surgeon. Better to leave before they arrived. It was one thing for them to think I had killed the man, but to perhaps discover something else upon examination of the body...

No one intercepted us in the passage, nor at the door. It had been a long time since I had opened a door for myself and I stifled a giggle, sure I must be going mad.

"Your Highness. Your Majesty," said Koto as we stepped out into the chill night. It had started to snow, light flakes settling upon the guards' helmets. The palanquin's oiled cover sagged beneath the growing weight, but as Takehiko climbed onto the mounting block the carriers pulled it tight to bounce off the snow. "Back to the palace, Your Majesty?"

"Yes, Koto. And quickly. Prince Takehiko is tired."

"Yes, Your Majesty."

He wanted more, but now was not the time. Too many eyes. Always too many eyes.

Brushing aside the curtain with my unbloodied hand, I

climbed in after Takehiko, grateful for the dark, close comfort the vehicle afforded. Takehiko had already curled up upon the furs, but this time he was facing the other way, his head in the lap of another. A cry for the guards froze to my tongue.

"Your Majesty," a deep voice said as the palanquin rose with a jolt.

"Nyraek," I said, and for a brief moment my heart soared. "I see you retain the loyalty of my guards. I might have to speak to Koto about that."

"Koto was my second too long to give his loyalty to another."

The observation that the only person Koto would ever give his loyalty to was himself, I left unspoken. "That must keep you warm at night."

A moment of silence fell, but without being better able to see his face it meant nothing. "How is General Kin managing in my place?" he said as the palanquin picked up speed.

"Well enough," I said. "His Imperial Majesty takes him everywhere and leaves Koto to guard the rest of us."

Nyraek grunted. "A mark of favour indeed," he said, a bitter note there though perhaps only because it was expected. I had wished for him often since his exile, wished for someone to share my burdens and to hold me when fear came in the night, but the Emperor had taken that away, too.

Silence remained as we passed through the narrow streets, and though the darkness hid his face it also hid my troubles. And Lord Epontus's blood. Soon enough a passing light allowed a glimpse of handsome features, but his eyes were downturned to the sleeping boy in his lap.

There his hand patted the curls seemingly without thought.

"I've heard you take him with you often," Nyraek said once we returned to darkness.

"You mean Koto tells you I take him with me often," I said. "I think perhaps I need a new head guard."

"Don't play that game with me, Li."

"What game?"

"The high and mighty empress."

I drew myself up. "It might have slipped your memory, Nyraek, but I *am* a high and mighty empress."

"Not for much longer, I hear. No, not Koto this time. There are whispers. Just as there were always whispers about us. About..." His hand stilled in the boy's hair. "You have to stop using him, Li."

"Why? He knows when people are lying and that is something I need to know."

"I know why you take him, but you have to stop. You might be able to convince some that you are just a devoted mother, but since you never took Yarri or Tanaka anywhere with you, at best they will think you are more devoted to Takehiko because he is not Emperor Lan's son."

My heart thudded as hard as it had back in Lord Epontus's sitting room. "Prince Takehiko Otako is the son of the Great Emperor Lan Otak—"

"Don't give me that kasu, Li."

"He was formally accepted. It is signed."

"And well for him, but I know my own blood as does anyone else who looks at him." Nyraek lifted one of the boy's arms and drew back the silk sleeve. A birthmark stood upon fair skin – three horizontal lines crossed by a diagonal. He had been schooled never to show it. Ever. "It is fine while he is young," Nyraek went on allowing the sleeve to fall back. "But he will only get stronger and once he is old enough to form lasting memories you risk him Maturating. He needs to be with me."

I suppressed the instinct to grip Takehiko's arm. "No," I said. "He is an Otako and needs to be with his mother."

"Li—"

"How is your son, Lord Laroth? He must be nearing manhood now, surely."

"Twelve, I think."

"You think?" I laughed, hating the brittle cruelty. But I needed to hurt him, to spill my fear and anger before it consumed me. "You cannot even look after one son. Why would I let you have mine, too?"

By this time we had reached the broader streets about the palace where strings of lanterns hung overhead, bringing diffuse light to our silk-hung hideaway. It etched a scowl upon his handsome face, a scowl I remembered all too well. For years it had been there, always watching, always protecting. I could not pinpoint the moment it had changed, when he had begun to linger, when I had smiled, when the times the Emperor didn't need the commander of his Imperial Guard had become joyous meetings hidden away from the court and its prying eyes. But there are always people watching, listening, whispering, and when I grew heavy with child again I was not the only one who doubted.

"You're afraid," he said, breaking the silence. "Why?"

"Don't you dare do that to me."

His scowl deepened. "It never bothered you before. Why now? Are you hiding something from me?"

The question meant that for all his loyalty Koto had told him nothing. I could tell him about the seer, but he would only laugh. He might then put his arms around me, might take the fear away with a touch of his hand, but that would not stop the march of fate.

"You have been away too long," I said, letting my gaze drift to the necklace that hung free of his tunic – an elaborate eye he'd commissioned from the imperial jeweller. What had once comforted seemed now to mock.

"I did not go because I wished to. I went because my Emperor commanded me to go. He would have killed me had I stayed, might still do so now if he finds out I'm here." He spread his arms wide. "See how much I trust you? I am wholly at your mercy."

"Hardly. He would just use it as an excuse to execute us both. I think you knew that when you came. I don't need your strange sight to see some of what you see."

He bowed his head, the gesture was respectful and yet mocked like the eye pendant. He had always been contradictory. "Perhaps I did know that, but that doesn't mean I don't trust you. Tell me why you're afraid."

"Because I don't want to die."

The palanquin ducked back into darkness and halted. "Your Majesty," came Koto's voice through the silk. "We are near the gates."

"I have to go," Nyraek said, gently shifting the still sleeping Takehiko off his lap. "But I'll be in touch. And though I am no longer formally the commander of your guard, I promise nothing is going to happen to you while I am alive to protect you. Yes?"

He gripped my hand, and though he frowned as I tucked the other into my sash he said nothing. Like sunlight spreading over my skin, a warmth of reassurance chased the chill of fear, its price the tightening of his features and the grim set of his jaw. An exchange.

He let go, waited, but all I could do was nod and chase

his retreating form with a smile. Yet despite the warmth he had gifted, my smile faded once the curtain fell back into place. Fear eked back.

"It's too late for that," I whispered as the palanquin moved on. "You were gone too long."

THE SOUND OF THE SERVANT BRINGING FRESH COALS IN THE morning did not wake me because I was not asleep. Footsteps. The thud of the fuel box. Then scraping. Curled up beneath my feather duvet, I watched dawn light sprinkle through the decorative shutters to fall like snow.

No one had seen us return, Koto too well used to organising secret trysts to fail now. Takehiko had gone sleepily off to the nursery while I hissed warnings in Koto's ear. Epontus had not been persuaded. He had been a threat and I had killed him. It was all he needed to know and he had taken it with a bow and a grim nod of satisfaction. He had wanted to bring the ministers in at the beginning. Now he would get his chance.

More scraping. A shuffling step as the servant moved around, trying to be as stealthy as an assassin and failing. I rolled. And sucked in a breath as the tip of a knife came to rest upon my throat. The mat had been empty but for me, yet now a chest heaved its breathlessness against my back, while at my ear a voice said: "Silence is the wisest course, Your Majesty," his words hot upon my skin. "Anything else might see you have an accident like Lord Epontus."

I froze, sure even a breath would cause the knife to pierce my skin.

"Good."

The arm let go, and freed I sat up, spinning to face my

assailant. "You!" I backed away, chill air nipping at my skin. "How did you get in here?"

"My secret." Gadjo put back the hood of his cloak, and although it was forbidden he kept his gaze brazenly upon me, a lilt to a pair of full lips. "I thought you might wish to see me," he went on when I did not speak. "Which is good because I wanted to see you."

I glanced at the knife and, seeming to notice, he lifted it along with his brows. "Worried about this? I'm not planning to use it on you unless I have to. Like you, Your Majesty, I must protect myself. That is, after all, why you killed my master."

"I didn't kill him. He fell."

"On to a knife. In your hand. Yes. I saw." He laughed. "You think servants don't spy when they are sent from the room? There was probably a whole gathering of them outside the doors on your wedding night."

"That is disgusting!"

"That is the payment we take for doing the bidding of our masters all day and all night."

His leer turned my stomach. The emperor was not the only man I had lain with, and no matter how careful Nyraek and I had been whispers had still gotten out. "What do you want from me?"

Gadjo lowered the knife and ran a hand through his short silvery hair, thick like the coat of a wild animal. "I want your son."

"My son?"

"The boy, Takehiko."

"What do you mean you want him? He is a Prince of Kisia not a loaf of bread."

His silver brows lifted. "No? Do you really think he will be welcome here once the Emperor gets rid of you? He is...

difficult, I hear. Different. A freak. All rumours set about by your enemies, of course," he added, lifting his hands to placate my maternal rage. "But I saw what he did last night and I do not think it will be long before he is... quietly removed from the palace. Sent north, perhaps, to his uncle where he can lead a quieter life. But of course his carriage will be attacked on the way and the emperor will have to announce the sad news that his youngest son did not survive. Such a pity. So sad. But perhaps by then another child will be on the way, growing in the belly of Lady Jingyi Matoda."

My hands clenched into fists, the fine nails Zuzue tended cutting into my palms. "You speak filthy lies."

"I am merely prophesying a future that can yet be altered."

"Who are you?"

"Gadjo, a most loyal servant of Lord Epontus of Chiltae."

"No servant can get in here without being seen. No servant looks an empress in the eye and speaks of her son's death. I could have you killed. Who are you?"

"I am Gadjo."

Assuming he still lived, the Imperial Guard outside my door would hear me if I screamed, but not before Gadjo stuck that blade in my neck.

"Then I thank you for the warning, Gadjo," I said. "But I am capable of protecting my own son. You may now leave by whatever method you arrived."

He sat his knife upon my buckwheat pillow. "I do not leave without your son."

My laugh was weak. Fearful. "Do you plan to just walk into the nursery and take him?"

"He is still in the nursery?"

42

Stupid. "He spends some of his time there," I said, trying to claw back from the precipice. "Juno is one of the few people who can manage him."

"And you."

"And me."

"Then I should take one of you with me."

I tried for my own sneer. "He will not go anywhere with you. And the guards would kill you before you ever set foot in the room."

"Perhaps. But I'm here, am I not? It is possible you are not so well guarded as you think."

I folded my arms to hold in my rising panic. "Then why not just walk over there and take him?" I said, voice shrill. "Why come to see me at all?"

Those hateful brows rose again, all mocking laughter. "It would be rude not to let you know my intentions. He is your child and you are, after all, the empress. At least for now."

"Well you have told me, now go."

Gadjo spun the knife upon my pillow. "You don't think I can."

"No, I don't."

"But you're afraid I will."

I kept my answer trapped, afraid of its power.

His lips split into a broad grin. "It does me good to see you afraid. To see the great Empress Li brought down to the level of mere mortals." Gadjo rose from my mat then and I reached out as though to stop him, his only response a laugh. "And some maternal instincts. How lovely. But if you do not give me your son you will wish last night's work undone."

"My son for your silence, is that the deal?"

His smile widened like a wild lion. "Something like that, yes."

"Why do you want him?"

"Who doesn't want a boy who can kill with a touch and not leave a trace?"

Not leave a trace. Truly the perfect assassin. If the emperor found that out then a whole different future might stretch before the boy, not one in which he was quietly removed, but in which he was put to good use. I hardly knew which was worse.

"No," I said. "You cannot have him."

Gadjo bowed then, picking up his knife from my pillow. "Then you do not have my silence and soon you will see how dangerous a servant can be. You're welcome to double the guard about your son or try taking him somewhere I won't find you, but I can tell you now it is wasted effort. I will always find you. And I will be back."

"How can—?

My jaw snapped shut. But for a lingering scent of dusty parchment and damp autumn leaves, the room was empty. The door had not slid upon its track, but I could almost believe the heavy curtain that hung before the balcony trembled.

I rushed to the nursery, heedless of the interested glances I met along the way. There Juno paced the floor soothing Princess Hana's gusty cries, while Takehiko lay curled in a pile of blankets playing with an abacus. Click. Click. Click. He did not look up, but as I drew closer so the clicking sped.

"Your Majesty!" Juno bowed with Princess Hana still in her hands, one of her fat cheeks lying upon her nurse's shoulder. Her little face was red and blotchy and her nose wet. "I'm sorry, Your Majesty, I was not expecting you."

The woman's eyes darted about the untidy floor, the wooden horses no doubt left there by Rikk who wanted to be a soldier when he grew to manhood. "Quick girl, clean them up," she hissed, waving a hand at the maid who helped her. "Then run and fetch some tea for Her Majesty."

"There is no need," I said, my gaze sliding back to Takehiko. All he had done was touch the man. Lord Epontus dead without even a grunt of effort. "I just came to see how my children are today."

"Her Highness is cutting a tooth and is very unhappy about it, Your Majesty," Juno said, bouncing the blotchy, damp baby when she started to whimper again. "Only Takehiko was more upset when he cut his first tooth. Yarri barely noticed, but then he is such a strong boy."

The clicking of the abacus beads quickened. "Yes," I said, thinking of the boy that was almost a man now. The boy who would cast me off as his father had done. "Prince Yarri is very like his father," I said in a dead tone. "Tanaka, too."

"You should be very proud of them both, Your Majesty."

"I am proud of them all." I walked toward Takehiko's refuge. "I will have a moment alone with my son."

"Of course, Your Majesty, I shall see if the princess is ready to sleep."

I waited until the door slid closed before I knelt, close enough to touch him though I kept my hands upon my knees. The abacus beads clicked back and forth in time with the rapid hammering of my heart. Just a touch.

"Takehiko?"

The boy's sandy hair lay tangled against the blanket, his eyes staring at nothing.

"Takehiko?"

He looked up and the snap of the beads ceased. "Yes, Mama?"

Words failed to come. How could you ask a child how he had killed a lord?

"Mama?" The beads started clicking again though he wasn't looking at them now. "You are afraid. Very afraid. Of me?"

"Not of you, my darling," I said, torn by the worried crease between his brows. "I know you would never do anything to hurt me. But..."

"Do you want me to kill the person who is making you scared again?"

Such wide, innocent eyes. It ought not to be his job to protect me, or to protect himself, but Gadjo had gotten in without being seen and disappeared again as though he had never existed. There was no saying when he would return or how, and when he did...

"There is a man," I said, each word slow as though they wished not to be spoken. "The servant from last night." I swallowed hard. "Gadjo, is his name. He is going to try to take you from me. You must not let him."

"No, Mama. I won't."

Again the clicking stopped and a small smile mirrored my own. "You are not so afraid now. That makes me happy."

"Takehiko..." I looked down at my hands clasped upon my knees, pale stones upon a bed of scintillating silk. "How did you do it?"

"I gave him your fear."

"Gave him my..." I met those wide eyes then. "What do you mean you gave him my fear?"

46

"You were very scared, Mama. You wanted him dead. So I killed him."

The simplicity of his words made it all the more chilling and I suppressed a shudder. But he would feel my disquiet though I did not recoil, would hear the race of my heart though I appeared calm. Nyraek had warned me of that, but not of this. Dead because I had wanted it so.

"Takehiko?"

"Yes, Mama?"

"Could you... do it for anyone else?"

His brow crinkled. "But you are my Mama."

"Yes, my darling, I am."

"There is only one Mama."

My relief sparked another of his fleeting smiles. "And only one Takehiko."

"WE HAVE NO CHOICE NOW," KOTO SAID, KEEPING HIS VOICE to a low growl as he paced the matting. "Cheng will not like it. But we are the last bastion of defence Kisia has left. Whatever the people believe, soldiers always know the truth. We were losing the last war and we will lose this one, doubly so when our new *allies* turn on us."

"I agree," I said, though my thoughts were back in the nursery with Takehiko. Killed with a touch. No mark left upon the skin. Nothing. And there he sat with his sandy hair and the round innocent face of a child little older than an infant.

Koto cleared his throat. "Your Majesty?"

"Yes, Koto?"

"I said it will have to be you who speaks to them."

"Speaks to who?"

His frown snapped into place. "The ministers, Your Majesty. Our next step."

"Yes, of course." The ministers. Both were old allies of the Otakos. It would be dangerous, risking it all on the belief they knew nothing of the secret alliance, that they would not want this war. But the emperor was the emperor. In order to stop this he would have to be... replaced. Once a difficult task, but now...

"There will have to be a coup," I said, more to myself than to Koto. "With Tianto in Koi the timing is good. He cannot take part in what he does not know."

"Yes, Your Majesty, and if you had been listening I said that one of your sons..." Koto left the words hanging.

"One of my sons." I fiddled with the lid of the teapot while Koto went on pacing. "And if Yarri refuses? If Tanaka refuses? If even Rikk sides with his father?"

A pause. "Then there is always Takehiko."

"Yes, there is always Takehiko. But to make enemies of my sons..." It was my turn to leave the words hanging, not wanting to finish the sentence though its conclusion filled my mind. To make enemies of my sons would end with their deaths or mine. But it didn't have to be that way. If there was no emperor to side with.

Koto stopped pacing. "To be a leader is to make hard decisions, Your Majesty. If Prince Yarri would ally himself with pirates and barbarians and start a war that could destroy Kisia, would you let him?"

The man had a piercing stare when he chose and I found I could not meet it. My mind said no, but my heart cowered from what that meant. To rid Kisia of an emperor grown too arrogant, too cruel, who truly believed himself a god – that would have satisfaction to walk with the bittersweet. But my children. Yarri was barely yet a man.

"Would you?"

"I don't know."

Koto grunted. "The truth at least. You had better hope the question doesn't arise then, for if you won't kill, I will. I have come too far to step back now."

"I understand. I will talk to him."

"Too risky. He might warn the emperor. No. To the ministers first. Without them there can be no coup. Even with so many of the Imperial Guard still loyal to Lord Laroth, it's the ministers who hold the power."

I nodded, his words adding to the brewing plan clouding my thoughts. There was only one way to protect Kisia, to protect myself and all of my children. The emperor had to die. But he had to die secretly. There and gone as though removed from history without becoming a martyr or a hero. Just a corpse. But it was one thing for my hand to strike, another to give the job to a child.

"Give me a day's grace, Koto," I said. "To let things cool. Then I will send Zuzue to Minister Tarli. Best to see the Minister of the Left first in the circumstances, I think."

"I agree. But take care. The court is rife with gossip about Lord Epontus."

"What do they say?" Zuzue had already given me an account, but it was worth hearing it from his lips.

Koto shrugged. "The usual speculation. As he was not here as an official ambassador people seem keen on the idea that he fell foul of a common whore, or some other dark dealing, but the Chiltaen ambassador is demanding answers."

"Of course. Had there been another way I would—"

Scowling, Koto lifted his hand, an ear pricked toward the door. "Majesty, I think—"

The door shot open, bouncing in its track. General Kin

stood in the aperture, afternoon light shining upon his customary scowl.

"General," I said, drawing myself up to full haughty empress though I wished to sink into the floor. "You were not given permission to enter."

He bowed, not the graceful bow he had given me outside the emperor's apartments, but the brusque economical bow of the angry soldier. "Forgive me, Your Majesty," he said, the words like the staccato snap of sandals on stone. "I shall be gone in a moment. Captain Koto is under arrest."

"Why?" I said.

Koto drew himself up and scowled at his commander, but said nothing.

"On a charge of treason, Your Majesty," General Kin said. "For aiding in the death of Lord Epontus of Chiltae."

"Aiding in the death—"

General Kin spun his ferocity upon me. "Your presence is also required by His Imperial Majesty."

"My presence?"

"Yes, Your Majesty. At once." He looked at Koto, a brief glance of disgust and annoyance, before gesturing to the guards behind him. "Take the captain away."

Still Koto did not speak. He was armed, but drew neither sword nor dagger upon his comrades, letting them bind his hands and lead him away. But where there might have been defeat there was pride, and where pleading eyes might have turned my way he did not risk a look lest he give away more than they knew. Let him be just another guard to me, nothing more.

THE THRONE ROOM WAS EMPTY OF ALL BUT ECHOES. EMPEROR Lan sat upon the Crimson Throne and watched my approach, no Jingyi this time, no court, nothing but the haze of red-tinted light that spread in through the stained-glass windows.

At my back walked General Kin, his heavy footfall muted compared to the snap of my sandals. I stopped and bowed at the Humble Stone and there I waited, head to the floor, until the emperor bade me rise.

"You always were a stupid woman," he said as I got to my feet. Sitting upon the great lacquered throne I could see why people thought him a god. But I knew better. I had seen him make love, grunting like a pig, had seen him sit upon the chamber pot and sleep with drool sticking to his lip. He was a man like any other, except unlike any other he needed to die.

I buried that thought as deep as I could.

"Stupid and more trouble than you were ever worth," he said, his voice filling the room. "You know," he added, shifting position upon his throne. "I could have had you executed after you birthed the bastard, but I chose not to. People would have said I could not control my own wife. They would have whispered. They would have talked. They would have laughed. So I accepted the boy as my own kin and let you stay. And your thanks for my forbearance? A daughter and treason."

Emperor Lan rose from the Crimson Throne and stood looking down at me, lips twisted to a sneer. "You may leave us now, General," he said. "Prepare to execute the traitors. A warning must be given to those who think to betray me."

"Yes, Your Majesty."

I did not turn, just listened as General Kin's tread

retreated toward the great doors. They creaked as they opened and creaked as they closed, shutting me in. Beyond the crimson windows snow dusted the branches of skeletal trees in the garden and the walls of the outer palace beyond.

"You see, my dear," Emperor Lan said, striding to the dais steps. "Eight men are going to die because of you. Eight guards who were only doing what they were told. I shall be sure to send their heads to their families with your compliments."

Koto, his neck still bloody and his eyes staring. But at who? I didn't even know what family he had, knew nothing about him except that he had given everything for Kisia, and for his ambition. Even his life. There might yet be a chance to save him if I said the right things, if I took the blame for it all. But where would that end?

The emperor stepped onto the smooth black floor and made his way toward me. "Still nothing to say?" he said. "I could suggest something perhaps. How about you beg? Get down on your knees and beg for forgiveness, beg for your life to be spared, beg for mercy or pray to whatever wretched god you heathens believe in."

I did not kneel.

"No?" he came across the floor as a beast stalks prey. "At least I have taught you pride."

Emperor Lan stopped before me and it took all my control not to step back. There was nowhere to run. "The Chiltaen Oligarch, Lord Epontus is dead," he said, leaning close enough that his warm breath touched my face. "This, as I imagine you can see, does not look good. Easy enough to say it was an accident, but there will always be whispers. And people live and die upon the tide of whispers."

He struck me, the force whipping my neck, but I held my ground.

"You seem to be lost for words," he went on when I did not speak. "I said before that it would not have looked good to execute you, but I might still do so if you provoke me. Lord Epontus is dead. Why?"

Why? A chance then that he did not know.

A slap returned the other way, not as strong with his left hand but unexpected enough that I staggered. "You ordered him killed. Why?"

"He had plans to force the other oligarchs into another war," I said, keeping my hand from touching my cheek though it smarted. "He offered me asylum."

No slap this time, just a growl. "You think I'm stupid enough to believe that? If you were innocent you would have brought the matter to me. Now stop—" He struck me so hard I cried out and fell upon the hard floor. "—lying." Loose tresses hung over my face and I was glad of their protective curtain as I sat upon the black boards, the emperor stalking around me.

"You know what I think," he said, each step the slow beat of a death drum. "I think you went to him for help." He continued to circle. "I think you didn't like being sent away and went to the highest ranked Chiltaen you could find to beg for help. What did you want him to do? Start a war so you could keep your title? And when he refused? Well... he knew too much by then, didn't he?"

I watched his feet as I sneered behind the fall of my hair.

"And now eight of my guards are going to die for following your orders."

His foot dug into my side, not a hard kick but an insistent grind beneath the sharp edges of his wooden sandal.

"Aren't you going to beg for their lives? Women are soft-hearted. Are you not a woman?"

"They don't need to die," I said through gritted teeth.

Lan removed his foot. "Oh? Don't they? Then shall I execute you to sate the Chiltaens when they clamour for blood? It is tempting, I assure you. How terrible it would be for them to know he was killed by one of their own. You are on your way out. Hardly my responsibility anymore. Old. Desperate. It could make quite the story. Yes, almost you have convinced me."

No more pacing. He stood, one foot tapping now as he thought – a habit his council had long since urged him to cease. What god did such things?

To the beat of his tapping foot the room spun. Koto was going to be executed, and such could be my end too if the Emperor willed it. How the seer would be laughing in her grave. So many steps taken to ensure survival, and every one of them had brought death closer.

"Yes," he said at last, cutting through my haze. "The execution of the former Empress Li, daughter of Chiltae, and the removal of her bastard children from the succession might just sate their desire for justice."

"Why does it even matter?" I said, pushing back my hair to glare up at him. "You are just going to start the war again anyway using the Curashi. Just claim Lord Epontus attempted to kill you and send your barbarians in."

Not a jab this time but a kick, his sandal slamming into my ribs with a swish of crimson silk. Grimacing, I sought for breath, only for the kick to come again. My shoulder. My back. My side. However I tried to protect myself he struck, layering bruises upon bruises until I curled against the barrage, tears and mucous dampening my sleeves.

When at last he stopped I did not move. Silence ruled

the throne room, the only sound that of my breath inside my protective shell.

"Who told you?"

"I listen."

He kicked my back. I whimpered.

"Who told you?"

"I listen."

A kick to the same place, this time eliciting a yowl I could not contain. I wanted him to stop. I wanted to be far away. But more than anything I wanted back the Lan who had loved me once.

"Their emissary, Irash," he said. "That was you, too."

I didn't answer. Braced for the kick.

"Who killed him?" He gripped my forearms and yanked me up, and though I kicked and fought and screamed, he was stronger. He twisted both of my arms until I could not move, could barely breath. "Who killed him?" he asked again, so close his chest heaved against mine.

"Who are you protecting? Laroth?"

My laugh surprised even me and brought a scowl to his brows. "What is so funny?"

"You think Lord Laroth gives a damn about what you do? *I* killed him. *Me*. With my own hands. Now what are you going do about it? The Curashi drop traitors off tall cliffs, but you're already planning to behead me for the Chiltaens, so who is it more important to please?"

"You?"

He did not let go, but neither did he tighten his grip.

"You're surprised? You stopped protecting me a long time ago."

"Protecting you? That's what we have guards for you stupid woman."

I laughed. There was relief in being so far beyond redemption it didn't matter what I said. "That isn't the same and you know it."

Lan shoved me away and I staggered, arms stinging. "I ought to have listened when the council said it was foolish to take a Chiltaen bride," he said. "You have caused me nothing but trouble." He began to pace the floor, scowling at his feet as they peeped from beneath the skirt of his grand crimson robe with every step. He ought to have been shouting, ought to be hitting me, demanding to know why I had done it, how, and with whose help. Yet those questions did not come.

"The guards will be executed in the morning," he said, muttering as though I no longer existed. "The Chiltaen ambassador must be there. Yes. And Li—" he looked at me then. "You will admit your wrongs, admit being unfaithful and birthing a bastard, and retire to a sanctuary in the south where you can do no more harm. Takehiko will be disinherited and you may take him with you for all I care, although to ensure you do not flee to Lord Laroth he will be recalled for duty. This is my decree."

"But I killed two men." *More than two*. But the rest had died for other reasons at other times.

No longer pacing he strode toward me, but no strike came, no kick, no snap of my bones in his grip. "I am an emperor. A god," he said. "I cannot be wrong. I can do no wrong for everything I decree is right. It cannot be that you killed men behind my back. It cannot be that you committed treason. It cannot be that such things were done without my knowledge because I know all. You will admit your weakness as a woman and retire. And this is the last time I ever want to see you."

His words stole my breath as surely as had the tip of

his sandal. After trying so hard to evade death it hurt to have it snatched from me, to have that certainty removed and replaced with a future I could not see. A future in which death would be allowed to creep up on me whenever it chose.

You will die before your thirtieth year.

"But... Your Majesty—"

Your children will die.

He sneered. "Now you want to beg?"

And Kisia will burn.

"No, the seer—"

"Is that why you betrayed me?" His sneer grew uglier. "Was it not enough to have the woman burned? Get out before I change my mind and execute you with the others."

This wasn't supposed to happen. But I had been given my life, allowed to leave, so I did the only thing that made sense. I knelt and bowed, and a fierce spark of joy lit my heart as I did, knowing it would be the last time. But before I went I would make sure he regretted his mercy. Though I might not be her empress anymore, I would not let Kisia burn for the whim of any god.

"Goodbye, Your Majesty," I said when he gave permission for me to rise. "Long live Emperor Lan."

THE SNOW FELL SOFT BEYOND THE LACEWORK SHUTTER, ITS tiny holes letting in biting winter air. Quite a crowd had gathered in the Divine Square, a silent, shivering crowd blanketed in fear. No, not fear, not yet. Fear would come later, supplanting the anxiety that twisted in their guts like snakes. The last war had started the same way. With strange deaths and executions.

From my high vantage in the outer palace I could see the stage and upon it the players walked. Emperor Lan seated upon a wooden copy of the Crimson Throne with Jingyi beside him, the Chiltaen ambassador, the Minister of the Left, the Minister of the Right, and a whole bank of Imperial Guards there to keep the commoners from their god. And because such things are all about the spectacle there were eight blocks upon the platform. Eight blocks with eight headsmen. And dusted in snow the people of Mei'lian watched on, each clutching a desperate wish to their heart that this would not be the beginning of the end.

I heard the steps behind me but did not turn. Something in the creak of leather and the heavy tread warned me who it would be, and on the air the scent of sweat and oil.

"Why do people watch?" I said, not turning from the play unfolding beneath me.

"Curiosity, Your Majesty," said General Kin, silk swishing as he bowed. "And perhaps for some the joy of seeing death."

"Is that why you became a soldier, General?"

"No, Your Majesty. A soldier fights so others do not have to."

"A worthy sentiment."

He didn't say anything, didn't move, yet his presence weighed upon my attention, and I turned. His usual scowl was absent, leaving, if not a handsome face, at least a distinguished one, with a pair of dark eyes that always watched, windows to a mind that always turned. Most men at court were liars and schemers, pompous and self-important. Kin ought to have been. He had a position of great power, had the emperor's ear, and yet his sneers were only ever directed at himself. In another life perhaps it might have been worth knowing him better.

"His Majesty is in the square," I said, when still he did not speak. "Ought you not be with him?"

"He is well guarded, Your Majesty. He informed me that you would soon be departing and so I have come to offer some of my men as an escort to ensure your safety."

Bitterness trembled in my smile, I knew, but I could hide it no longer. "Imperial Guards are only for the Imperial Family, General," I said. "Since in a few days the council will declare me no longer the Empress of Kisia and my shame will be paraded before the people, I do not think I will be requiring the services of His Majesty's guards."

No blink of surprise. "Not then perhaps, but if you were to go now, today, I would personally see to it that you and Prince Takehiko are escorted by my finest men."

"Koto was one of your finest men."

There was yet no sign of him outside, only a patchwork of snow upon the platform. As though part of a ceremony, eight headsmen were sharpening their axes.

"Yes," General Kin said. "He was. But he made a poor choice."

I snorted a laugh. What was it Koto had said? "To be a leader is to make hard decisions," I said, and wondered whether he still thought it was true in the shadow of death.

"Yes, Your Majesty, but I am his commander and so they are my decisions to make. I could have a carriage and a contingent of men ready to depart this afternoon."

"This afternoon?"

No clue to his thoughts permeated his expression, but

his gaze held mine with an intensity that made my skin tingle. For a mad moment I considered telling him about the secret alliance, but if anyone already knew it was Kin. He went everywhere with His Majesty – the emperor's man to whatever end.

I could not hold his gaze, could not face the unbending assurance of the soul that looked out at me.

"No," I said, turning back to the window. "There is still something I need to do before I leave. Perhaps I will be ready tomorrow, or the following day, but not today."

"As you wish, Your Majesty." Though he bowed his scowl returned. "I do hope you will change your mind. Mei'lian is not likely to long be a... friendly place."

"I do believe you are right, but I will stay nevertheless."

General Kin bowed again and would have departed, but I said: "Tell me, General, before you go. I... I have not seen Cheng this morning though he is usually one of my guards."

Once again I had expected surprise only to be disappointed. "He will be honoured to hear that you asked after him, Your Majesty."

That quelled the worst of my fears. "Cheng was one of the first Kisians I ever met, General," I said. "He served as part of my escort from Chiltae to Mei'lian as a bride, and was the only one who spoke to me like I was a person, rather than just a... a... thing that needed to be safely delivered."

Kin remained silent, his hands clasped, but again his expression grew intent and I found I could not hold it. "I would hate to know something unfortunate had befallen him due to this mess."

"Then I am pleased to be able to inform you that he has been reassigned, Your Majesty. Best you leave it there."

"Perhaps as a kindness to me you would consider making him one of the party that is to travel with me upon my journey south, as it is to be my last."

A beat of silence. Then: "Of course, Your Majesty."

This time he didn't immediately bow, didn't turn, but lingered. A moment. Two. Stretching on until the silence grew awkward. How easy it would be if I could turn him into an ally, but the risk was enormous. If he was even half as loyal to the emperor as I thought then the chance of surviving such an admission was miniscule.

"Something else to say, General?" I said.

He parted his lips to speak only to press them shut again and shake his head. "No, Your Majesty."

"Then that will be all."

I peered back through the shuttered window at the scene below and listened to his retreating footsteps. He halted once, prickling the skin on the back of my neck, but I did not turn, not until he was once again walking. Then I glanced over my shoulder at the retreating figure, tall and proud in his crimson surcoat, the tail of his sash dancing beside him. Without again looking back he turned a corner to be swallowed by the palace.

Outside the crowd had grown restless. It was too cold to be kept waiting so long, no matter how grand the spectacle. Were it not for the presence of their emperor they would probably have started throwing things to make the wait more interesting.

Silence fell in a heartbeat when Emperor Lan rose from his throne. He got to his feet, arms outstretched, his grand crimson robe shimmering in the weak morning light. Snow dusted his dark hair, but the people down in the square would not see that. They would only see the spikes of the Hian Crown atop his head, their eyes drawn to the dozens of jade charms that hung from it upon strings of gold as fine as spider thread. A gift from the gods to the Otakos – the ultimate symbol of divinity.

I sneered behind the safety of my shutter. A symbol of divinity forged by men. And in the name of those gods he would declare war upon Chiltae as soon as everything was in place.

The emperor spoke, but the whip of the chill wind kept his words from my ears. So rarely did he address his people that it was no wonder so many had come, as much to see their emperor in the flesh as to watch men die.

"Long live Emperor Lan!" the crowd cried, and that I heard, the combined strength of so many voices carrying far. "Long live Emperor Lan! Long live Emperor Lan!" It became a chant as the rhythmic beat of the death drum filled the square, only to fade voice by voice as new players climbed onto the stage. Eight guards this time, though stripped now of all that would once have identified them as the Emperor's men. No crimson sashes, no surcoats, no weapons – just eight men in plain grey robes so thin they might well freeze to death first. I hunted for Koto amid the group, but distance stole their identities leaving them eight figures in a flurry of snow.

A man in white stood amid the same fall of snow, and raised his hand to halt the drum. Father Kokoro, the court priest, recognisable where the others were not. Again I could not hear him, but I had heard the prayer enough times to need no guide.

"In the hands of the gods may you find true peace," I said. "In the hands of the gods may you find true justice.

May Qi guide you gently. His wisdom is great. His mercy everlasting."

Koto had known the risks, had known what he was doing, and yet I willed the world to change, to bend to my desires. Good men ought not die, ought not be cut down with so little honour.

"I used to think I was made to be an empress," I said to the shutter, not turning away though the eight men knelt. "Now I am not so sure."

Koto could have been any one of them, and since they all deserved my silent apology I looked to each in turn. The drum beat began again. Faster now. In his throne the emperor sat like the god he claimed to be, delivering justice, while safe behind my shutter tears coursed down my cheeks. "I'm sorry," I said. "It wasn't supposed to end like this."

The beat of the death drums sped to a crescendo. The executioners lifted their axes.

"In shadows we fight. In shadows we fall," I said, tears choking the words. "But it will not be in vain. History will remember."

It was my own prayer of a sort.

One of the axes fell before the last beat of the drum, dropping the first head. I could not hear the thwack of the heavy blade severing flesh, nor the thud as the head landed upon the wood, but I used to sit at the emperor's side and once you heard such sounds you never forgot them.

At the last beat the other seven axes fell. A few more heads hit the boards, but three axes lifted again for another strike. No cheer sounded, the crowd solemn as another head fell. But two were not fully severed and their executioners went again. It was butchery of the highest order, but I was as powerless as a sparrow. Beheading was not the Chiltaen way. We were people of the sea.

When at last the final axe hung silent I allowed myself to look away. Their souls had gone now, leaving behind only meat.

"You see what happens when you refuse me?"

No footsteps, no creak of floorboards, Gadjo was just there behind me as though he had always been there, a half smile upon his lips. Lips I wanted to rip off his face. "I see," I said, forcing down the rage. "But you have already seen the emperor and told him what happened with Lord Epontus, you can do nothing more to me now."

"See the emperor? Me? I am but a humble servant, Chiltaen, too, I am not allowed to do such things as be in the presence of your god."

"That doesn't alter the point. You are done."

I made to walk past him, but he gripped my arm, digging in his fingers. "I am not done. I am here to take the boy."

"Again you come to tell me so, why? Why not just walk into the nursery and take him?"

Gadjo sneered, but the moment of silence that filled the corridor was its own admission. "You can't," I said, before he could speak. "No, you're afraid to!"

He made no answer though I laughed, cruel joy in the sound. "You are too afraid to take him without permission because you've seen what he can do. Well you can take your demands and—"

"Be careful what you say, Your Majesty," he snapped. "If you think there is nothing more I can do to you then you are wrong. I have cut the string of one bow, but there are others you hold closer to your heart. Your sons could die. Your daughter. What mother would not trade one child for the safety of four?"

The words beat the breath from my lungs. "You would not get within reach of any of them before you were cut down," I said though he had crept up on me twice without a sound. Whoever he wanted dead would die.

Gadjo let go my arm and cooed in sympathy as I backed away. "I know it's hard to give up a child," he said. "But it is for the greater good, that phrase so beloved by the men who walk in god's shoes. You've tried, but though you stomp and shout no one hears you. But you're a woman, a mother, your heart bleeds and so you know that the greater good is subjective."

"Who are you?"

"I am Gadjo."

"And why are you doing this? Why do you want a boy who can kill without leaving a trace? What will you do with him?"

"Whatever needs to be done."

I snorted. "Who is stomping about in god's shoes now?"

He grinned. "A hit, Your Majesty, foolish of me to have underestimated my opponent."

"People do that, all men's thoughts seem to stop at breasts."

"I am not like most men."

"And so once again we find ourselves at the question. Why do you want him? And if you say who would not want a boy who can kill with a touch I will hit you."

His grin broadened. "You could try, but you would miss."

"That is not an answer."

Neither of us moved, our gazes locked in challenge.

65

Never before had fear created such anger, and as it thudded though me his smile began to fade. His eyes darted about my face. "You're not going to give him to me no matter what I say, are you?"

"No."

"Then you will get no answer. And I will keep taking from you until you change your mind."

"Then you will soon run out of things to take. And if you kill the emperor's son then you make an enemy of the Emperor of Kisia and that, I think, is not a smart plan. Whoever you are, he is stronger."

Again I made to walk past and again he gripped my arm. The sneer was back. "Perhaps. How about Kisia itself, Your Majesty? Would you give me Takehiko to save the people? From war, perhaps. From death and destruction?"

"Let go."

For a moment his fingers dug deep as though to bruise my skin, then he let go. A step back and he bowed. "Your Majesty. I will be back at midnight. You have until then to change your mind."

"I won't."

His smile was a hateful thing. "You will."

———

TAKEHIKO SAT ALONE IN THE NURSERY, AT ONE WITH HIS PILE of furs beneath the brazier. His abacus must have been hidden inside for its clicks escalated when I entered, like the increasing tempo of the death drums.

"Juno says we have to go away."

He didn't look up, but the simple words broke my heart. He had known no other home, yet Nyraek had been right. The Imperial Palace was no place for an Empathic bastard. So much trouble and all because I had thought myself in love.

"Yes, my love," I said. "Where is Juno?"

"She is talking to the nervous maid."

The clack of the abacus beads went on.

Glad of Juno's absence, I knelt upon the furs beside him. But my well-practiced words of explanation died beneath the stink of burned hair. "What is that—?"

A lump of black charcoal sat upon one of the fur blankets, a black ring of singed hair around it. "You ought not sit so close to the brazier," I said, shaking it off. It rolled a little way only to be stopped by its angular shape. "That could have landed on top of you."

"Juno says that is why I have to go away."

"Because a coal burned your furs?"

"Because I hurt people."

Still he didn't look up, but then he didn't need to. All he needed to know about people he felt with a different sense. I tried not to shiver. "That is nonsense, Takehiko. You—"

"I hurt Juno. And the nervous maid."

"What do you mean you hurt them?"

At last the clicking stopped, but the silence was no better. "I tried to pick it up, Mama," the little boy said, and held out the hand that had been sitting in his lap. It was bright red and blistered. "It hurt, but I didn't want it to hurt so I gave it away."

"Gave it—? Has the physician come?"

"Juno said she hoped it would swell up and kill me."

His words sent a chill blade through my heart and I got to my feet so fast I almost knocked the brazier over. Anger swirled about my steps like the silk of my skirt. "Juno," I

67

said, approaching the far door that led to the children's rooms. "Juno."

The door slid as I approached, forcing me to take a step back or collide with Juno. She stepped inside and closed the door. Then, with her nose in the air she stared at me and said: "Yes?"

"You forget yourself, Juno," I said, clutching at fading tendrils of calm. "Prince Takehiko requires a physician yet I understand you have not sent for one."

A sniff. "Takehiko is in no pain. His Majesty would not wish such a fuss made about nothing."

"Nothing? He has burned his hand!"

"The gods spare those of great faith."

No "Your Majesty", no bow, but then I was not the empress anymore.

"I see," I said, equally stiff. "I will see the princess now."

I went to walk past her, but Juno stepped into my path. "No."

"No? She is my daughter, Juno and you will stand aside."

"His Majesty's orders. I am to keep Princess Hana safe until you have departed Mei'lian."

"Don't do this, she is my only daughter, you must let me see her before I go. You must let me say goodbye."

She shook her head and kept her hand on the door-frame. "I'm sorry but I cannot."

I shouldered her out of the way. "Your Majesty!" she cried as I threw back the door, one of its taut paper panes snapping.

"Guards!"

No time. Heavy steps sounded to the beat of my own as I charged into the room. It was not large room but warm, the matting covered in tiger pelts, and upon their stripes sat the arched rockers of a wooden cradle. Despite the sound of pursuit the sight of my sleeping daughter slowed my steps. She lay still like a doll, her bottom lip tucked in as though in her dreams she suckled at the breast. Princess Hana, perfect from the wisp of blonde hair upon her head to the tiny fist she had formed in her sleep, and for an instant nothing mattered except the baby girl the Emperor would never again let me see – the daughter Gadjo had threatened to kill.

My own fists clenched as a hand closed upon each of my arms. Looking up I found the implacable faces of two Imperial Guards, neither known to me. Not Cheng. Not Koto. Not Nyraek. I was truly alone.

"I could not stop her," Juno gabbled. "She just pushed me out of the way."

I hoped the emperor would have her whipped.

"Bring the boy, too," one of the men said, jostling me through the doorway.

"Mama?"

The plaintive little voice mixed with the others and then, as though very far away, little Hana woke and started to cry. And I could not go to her. The guards tightened their grips on my arms and dragged me out into the passage. Takehiko started to wail, too, and tears dampened my cheeks.

I clenched my teeth upon words of fury. *I will fight you all. I will kill you all.*

Behind me a gasp ended in a strangled choke and I turned as best I could pinned between my jailors. One guard stood beside Takehiko, the other had fallen to his knees, juddering the boards. His breath came short and sharp, and with a hand pressed to his chest he toppled forward, hitting the floor face first and lying there still.

Shock reigned for a breathless moment. Then everyone shouted. The noise echoed along the passage, ringing my ears. Someone rolled the man over. Someone checked inside his mouth. Someone ran for the court physician. Someone repeated over and over that Sen had been just fine that morning. He must have choked. He must have been poisoned. He must have had something wrong inside. So much noise and not once did any of them look at Takehiko. The little boy stood silent beside his remaining guard, his lips moving as though muttering something under his breath.

Forgotten amid the chaos I stared at my son, fear settling like lead inside me. Lord Epontus had been one thing, but this... Perhaps it would be better to let Gadjo take him. Safer. Easier. Who better to raise a monster but another monster?

Takehiko looked up, hurt in his eyes though I had not spoken. A guard once more gripped my arm. "Get them out of here."

I allowed myself to be marched back to my apartments – apartments that would soon be redecorated and prepared for another as the nursery would be prepared for her children. That thought proved to be the breaking point, and in the safety of my room tears fell silent and bitter as the door closed us in.

Takehiko curled up in the corner. Zuzue went on folding a robe. A travelling chest already sat half full at her feet though I had given no orders. It seemed His Majesty had thought of everything.

"I am almost finished, Your Majesty," she said, bowing

to me, her sign of respect enough to make the tears fall faster. "It should be ready within the hour."

Within the hour. General Kin had wanted me to leave that afternoon. Perhaps he had wanted to save me from the humiliation of a dissolved marriage and the pain of parting from my children. Almost the prospect of safety in exile was tempting – somewhere to fade away and die in peace.

"Your Majesty." Zuzue bowed again. "Prince Rikk gave me this for you." She held out a roughly hewn wooden fish, no doubt meant to be an Otako pike had it been formed by stronger, more practiced hands. Tears blurred Zuzue's face as I held the sculpture as carefully as I would have held Rikk's heart.

"Thank you," was all I could say, but Zuzue had already returned to packing my robes. But I did not want to leave. I did not want to be sent away in disgrace. I did not want Kisia to break its treaty with Chiltae and be destroyed. So much had gone wrong.

Midnight.

I went to the brazier and held my hands over the coals, skin tingling. If I did not think of something in time I would have no choice but to let Takehiko go. I could warn General Kin, but Gadjo had already bypassed guards on two occasions and proved himself capable of all he threatened. Running was equally pointless. Getting Takehiko in to see Emperor Lan would solve one problem, but Gadjo would still come and His Majesty would see neither me nor my bastard son.

While Zuzue moved about the room, soft and silent, the pop and hiss of the glowing coals held me transfixed. Plans formed only to be discarded, each one left to hang about my head in a despairing haze. There were too many guards. Too little time. But whenever I considered giving up, the memory of Gadjo grinning reminded me that I would not be beaten.

"Zuzue?"

The woman stopped folding and bowed. "Yes, Your Majesty?"

"I need you to do something for me."

"Anything, Your Majesty."

"I wish to write a farewell message to Cheng and you will take it to him. It seems we are both to be leaving Mei'lian and I should thank him for his kindness."

Another bow. "Of course, Your Majesty."

She brought the lap desk and stirred the ink while I shook out a fresh piece of parchment and checked my brush for stray hairs. Throughout it all Takehiko did not move. I looked up every few seconds while I wrote, but still he did not move, barely even seemed to be breathing. Not for the first time I wondered what went on inside his head. If he could feel everything around him then the palace must be a noisy place.

I rolled up the finished message and held it while Zuzue lit the wax candle. Three drips. Four. Never again would I use the imperial seal whatever the outcome, so I took great care pressing the pikes into the wax. Too much care. The cold air hardened it fast, leaving it to crack around the edges as I pulled the stamp free.

It could not be fixed, so I handed it to Zuzue and with a bow she left, my heart pounding with the close of the door.

With nothing else to do but wait until midnight, I pulled my copy of Nyraek's eye pendant free of my robe and turned it over in my fingers. "Do not fail me now."

CHENG STOOD AT HIS POST IN THE GALLERY, BUT NO WELCOME softened his eyes. "Your Highness," he said, tight-lipped as he bowed to Takehiko before me. "Your Majesty."

"I am sorry to ask more of you, Cheng," I said, my hand upon Takehiko's shoulder though whether to protect him or everyone else I hardly knew. "You have been a good and loyal friend to me over the years, years in which I have imposed far too much upon you." He had kept more secrets than any man ought, had stood guard for us, had watched his commander's back, and now it had come to this.

"It is an honour to serve," he said, but when I grimaced he sighed. "It *has* been an honour to serve, but Kisia's future looks... messy from where I'm standing, and for the sake of my family I'm better out of it. I am an old man."

"Then I must thank you for your long service."

He grimaced again, filling his face with lines. "It is not quite done yet." He stood aside from the door and bowed again. "Please enter, Your Majesty."

The door to the little-used tearoom beckoned. Some misfortune of design had meant the sun never found its windows, leaving it cold and colourless. The perfect space for such meetings.

"He is here?"

"I am courting treason enough in my actions that I would rather not do so in words too, Your Majesty," he said, speaking low, an urgent note flurrying my heart. "Please enter."

"I will leave Takehiko here with you."

Cheng's countenance went wooden, but he nodded,

not looking at the boy. I squeezed Takehiko's shoulder. "Stay with Cheng and be good."

"He doesn't like me."

Cheng made a mumbled disclaimer, but I said: "Soldiers don't like anyone, that is how they stay good at their job. He will look after you though, for that is also his job."

"Yes, Mama."

I slid the door and chill air touched my face, scented with dust and old reeds. It might have been too dark had moonlight not eked in around the shutters to wallow like silver fog, encasing the kneeling form of Nyraek Laroth. Tightly-balled fists rested upon his knees, but he showed no other sign of disquiet.

"Your Majesty," he said, bowing as I entered.

No table, no cushions, just cracked reeds and an unlit brazier in one corner. We had made it comfortable once, back when he would have welcomed me with a smile. No smile now.

"You shouldn't be here," I said, a flicker of doubt halting my steps. "I should not have sent for you. You should go."

"No, I should not, but you wouldn't have asked for me if it was not important."

"But you are meant to be in exile. Who knows what he might do if he finds you here."

He. And to think I had been overjoyed when the emperor chose me from so many. I had dreamed a life of happiness and luxury, but as surely as Takehiko's birthmark marked him a bastard did my fair hair mark me as foreign, and little by little I had built tall defences.

Nyraek gestured to the floor in front of him. "Koto is dead. I'm not going anywhere until I know what is going on, so if you're worried about me being found then I suggest you join me."

Until Lord Nyraek had torn them down.

I knelt opposite him, this enigmatic, powerful man in whose arms I had once felt safe. He knelt with his knees spread, riding breeches visible beneath the fall of his silk surcoat. Once or twice I had seen him in full court robes, but he had been a fighter too long to return easily to the soft finery of a lord. An empty scabbard even hung from his belt. That he had worn it meant trouble, that it was empty meant the Imperial Guards who let him in had only trusted him so far.

My hands busied about the settling of my skirt, my eyes not meeting his.

"You are leaving the court," he said.

Not a question. "Yes."

"You take Takehiko with you?"

"Yes."

"If the emperor is disinheriting him then he should come to Esvar with me where he can be safe."

I had planned everything I wanted to say, but something about Nyraek's sharp gaze had always choked practiced lies before they were born. "Yes," I said. "He would be better off with you, raised with your son, but the emperor plans to recall you."

"I see." His eyes narrowed. "There's something else."

"There's a man," I said, the words struggling to come though I had practiced them over and over. "He... wants our son."

Our son. Words I had never spoken. Truth I had never admitted aloud.

"Who?"

"His name is Gadjo, a servant of Lord Epontus. He has

75

threatened to kill Yarri and Tanaka and Rikk and Hana if I don't give him Takehiko."

Nyraek laughed. "Your children are surrounded by guards, Li. They—"

"He got into my room without a single person seeing him. He got into the outer palace without a sound from the guards. He is the reason Koto is dead. Call me a foolish woman if you like, but this man will kill my children or take our son."

"How?"

"I don't know how he does it. He just seems to... appear and then disappear as though by magic."

Lord Laroth grunted. "I stopped believing in magic the day I Maturated. There is no magic there are only freaks."

"Then a freak is coming for our son at midnight and if I do not let him go he will kill the others, even little Hana. I cannot let that happen, Nyraek, you have to help me."

Any other man would have dismissed my fear, but not him. Not now.

"Midnight?" He looked toward the shuttered window, rimmed in moonlight. "An hour then, probably less. You ought to have sent for me sooner, but at least I'm here now. When this man comes he'll have to go through me."

Some weight ought to have been lifted from my shoulders, but the load only seemed to grow heavier. Then Nyraek said: "You had better tell me why he wants the boy."

And I could only shrug and shake my head, holding tight the truth lest he sense it in my thoughts. I trusted Nyraek with my life, but so had Emperor Lan, and Nyraek would not betray his emperor to a foul end whatever the cause. If Nyraek even suspected the whole of my plan it would be over before it began.

"He must have seen Takehiko's birthmark and realised he was special," I said, trying for dismissive. "Perhaps he thinks the boy could be trained to be useful."

Nyraek leaned forward. "Li, I don't need to be an Empath to know you're not telling me something. Something big. I don't want to take the truth from you, but I will if I must."

I threw myself back from him, but his hand never reached beyond his own knee. In a graceless tangle of silk, I righted myself some paces away. Too far for him to reach. He hadn't said a word. Hadn't moved. "If you dare to do such a thing I will inform His Majesty of your presence myself."

"You never used to be afraid of me."

"I am not afraid of you."

"Then why not tell me?"

Because you'll stop me. No, don't think that. Don't think that. "There is nothing to tell you, but all of this has me fearing my own shadow. I am to be thrown out in shame, Nyraek. Jingyi is to take my place." *Except that Lan will die first. He must die.*

His brow furrowed. "I know she is, but that felt like a lie."

"I said—"

"If you don't wish me to read you then don't throw your emotions around," he snapped. "Now look at you rubbing off on me. I wasn't agitated before you came in that door. If you want my help then I will give it, but I have to know everything. What are you so afraid of?"

I clasped my hands in my lap and took a deep breath, trying to exude only calm. It had been exhilarating in the beginning, knowing he could sense my emotions and touch my thoughts as he touched my skin, exhilarating to know the secret he kept from everyone, but now I had seen what Takehiko could do. Had seen him kill with little more than a thought.

Takehiko. I am scared of Takehiko.

"I am afraid for our son."

Nyraek lifted a hand only to think better of reaching out for mine. "Li," he said, crumpling it back into its fist. "I told you when he was born that Takehiko couldn't stay here, that we had a few years' grace, perhaps, time in which to make a plan to extricate him from His Majesty's influence. Those years have passed. This isn't the way I would have chosen to do it, but we have the opportunity to get him out of here and we need to do it now. I know he looks innocent, I know he's a child, but once he is old enough to understand, to form long-term memories, then he is old enough to Maturate. If he stays here beyond that he is either in grave danger, or the empire is."

His words froze the lie upon my lips. "What do you mean the empire is?"

"I mean that if the emperor realises what he can do he will either kill him, or use him. Using an Empath is a slippery, dangerous path, doubly so when that Empath is a child in whom no morals have been instilled. He has been brought up as a prince, as the son of a god, such a position breeds little empathy. And an Empath without empathy is—"

"A monster."

"Exactly. If he starts down that road there is no knowing where it will end. I don't yet know how powerful he will be. That is also the reason why no one can have him whatever they threaten. It is too dangerous."

He can kill with a touch. The words wouldn't come, the admission like a dagger to my own heart. I was the boy's

78

mother. Whatever he lacked was my fault. But the curse, as Nyraek called it, had come from his father.

He can kill with a touch.

"How powerful are you?"

Lord Laroth's brows rose. "You've never asked that question before."

"I never thought to. Answer it."

"I don't know," he said. "I have read histories of my family and in comparison I seem to be a poor wielder of the curse, perhaps because I have never wanted to use it. My father called it the curse because it killed my mother, so I spent half my life pretending it didn't exist. That's the only reason I managed to get by at court. What I allowed in was weak enough not to drive me insane."

He can kill.

"Then I think it is safe to assume Takehiko will be the same," I said. "And so you have no reason to fear anyone can use him for... evil means. How about your other son?"

"Darius?" there was a trace of a sneer. "He shows barely any sign of aptitude for anything, so I can only hope you are right. He is a very sickly boy, spends all his time playing Errant and reading."

"Then at least he will be no danger." Though I kept my distance I met Nyraek's sharp gaze. "If you can get Takehiko away from here without having to sacrifice my children then you may have him. But if you cannot I don't think I can do nothing and let a man kill my children."

"Even if it means handing a powerful weapon to an unknown enemy?"

"These are my children you are talking about," I said, my voice catching on a sob. "I cannot let them die."

"Is Takehiko not your child too?"

The softly spoken words stole my breath and stilled my heart.

"Yes," I said. "He is. Don't make me choose between them."

He is a monster.

"Li—" he reached out but I pulled my hand away.

"No," I said. "It is too late for that. My secrets are my own and if you will not help me then go."

"You have armoured yourself against me."

There was nothing to say. Silence passed in the grey light, every breath of cold air like knives in my throat.

"I see," he said at last, rising to stand before me. He bowed, just as he had as General Laroth of the Imperial Guard. The empty scabbard at his side seesawed. "Then it seems I have no choice but to stay until midnight. Where is Takehiko?"

Leaving Nyraek inside, I went to the door and slid it a little way open. Takehiko was sitting in the corner beneath a portrait of one of the emperor's ancestors. "Takehiko," I said. "Come."

The boy rose, and as he went past me into the room, I gripped Cheng's sleeve. "Go," I said. "Alert the guards that we are here."

"What? Lord Laroth—"

"Will be just fine, Cheng. Trust me."

"But Your Majesty, I—"

"You wanted to save Kisia," I hissed. "If you don't do this then we will have failed. In honour of Koto, go!"

He took a step only to look back, confusion crinkling his honest face.

"You have to trust me, Cheng. This is the very last thing I will ever ask of you. Go. Now. That is an order."

Cheng bowed then, his hands clenched tight. "Yes, Your Majesty."

With a racing heart I slid the door closed, shutting myself in with what remained of my family. Nyraek knelt before Takehiko, speaking to the boy though the boy made no answers. He shot a frown at me, full of silent question, but I used my long-perfected smile.

"We can wait here until the danger has passed," I said. "And in the morning I will order the carriage to take us away from here."

"Where are we going, Mama?" the boy said, coming to press his face into my skirt. "I don't want to go. I want Juno."

I kept the fingers in his hair calm, but the hand at my side clenched hard. "You don't need Juno anymore."

Nyraek stared very hard at me as though trying to read my mind – something I hoped he could not do.

"You are going to come to live at my estate in the country," he said to the boy. "It is much quieter there. You will meet my son, too. He is—" Nyraek took Takehiko's slack wrist and drew back his sleeve to see the birthmark. "—like you."

That made the boy look up from my skirt. "Like me?"

Nyraek had always worn a leather band tied around his wrist like an archer's bracer, but he untied it then under Takehiko's rapt gaze. In the faint moonlight it was hard to discern the line where his skin lightened, but the birthmark was impossible to mistake.

"You—" Takehiko looked up. "You're not afraid of me."

"No. I'm going to look after you."

Sure my heart would break if I watched them any longer, I turned toward the door. Midnight approached yet there was still no sign of Gadjo or the Imperial Guards. Had Cheng ignored my order?

"Perhaps we should leave now," I said. "Rather than waiting."

"No," Nyraek said while Takehiko traced the line of his father's birthmark with a finger. "If this man you mentioned wants to make a scene then better we keep away from untrustworthy eyes. Cheng I trust, but General Kin—"

Footsteps interrupted his words. At first they were soft like the distant patter of rain, only to rise to thunder as they approached. Nyraek swore and reached for his scabbard only to find it empty.

"Hide the boy," he hissed, squaring up before the door.

"Hide him? Where? The room is empty."

His eyes darted about but a second later the screen door slammed back upon its track and guards made faceless by shadows poured in. A dozen at least. One gripped my arm, but when another tried to touch Nyraek he shook them off with a snarl. "I can walk, Bahnu. I will walk. I am unarmed, as you see."

"Let him go, Bahnu," came the voice of General Kin. The man stood in the doorway, scowl in place. "Brave men walk to their own deaths."

"Ah, General Kin," said Nyraek. "I always said you would go far, but I did not expect you to rise to my position so soon."

"His Majesty has honoured me."

If anyone else heard Nyraek's snort they made no sign of it. "Indeed," he said. "There was a time he honoured me, too, so you had better watch your back."

"I am His Majesty's loyal servant. I am no threat. There

is no need for me to watch my back." He gestured to his men. "Bring them all. His Majesty is waiting."

It had been a gamble, but if anything could make Emperor Lan angry enough to break his own decree not to see me, it was the presence of Nyraek Laroth in his palace at my invitation. But as I was pushed out of the room behind Lord Laroth, new fears tempered my relief. With General Kin's grim gaze upon me I knew death waited.

You will die before you thirtieth year. Your children will die. The empire will burn.

We were in the hands of the gods now.

IT OUGHT TO HAVE BEEN THE THRONE ROOM – A GRAND STAGE for a final stand. Instead it was to the Emperor's apartments we were taken, General Kin ahead and an army of footsteps behind. Seeming to be fuelled by fury, the general moved at such a pace I had to drag Takehiko by the arm, but no matter the speed servants still stopped to whisper.

Nyraek scowled, not looking at any of the guards who had once been his men. They didn't look at him either, some perhaps the ones responsible for letting him in for one last tryst with his lady. Not until we approached the Emperor's apartments did Nyraek flick his scowl my way. I could risk no words, but just in case he could hear my thoughts I apologised in the silence of my head.

I'm sorry. This was the only way.

The general went in first, sliding the double doors closed behind him. Light bloomed through the thin paper along with low voices. Then the doors opened again spilling light upon us.

"Ah, Lord Laroth and Empress Li, my darling wife, do come in."

The emperor sat once more upon his grand chair, not in his full court robe but in a crimson dressing robe finer than anything most of his subjects would ever own. His long dark hair hung loose tonight, falling to his shoulders like a lion's mane. A hint of the animal glinted in his eyes too – bright and hungry as the guards led us forward to bow.

I did so, and cared nothing for how long he kept us with our foreheads pressed to the reeds. Each moment he thought to bestow humiliation only brought midnight closer.

"Rise." Emperor Lan grunted as we got to our feet, his eyes having drifted to Takehiko. "I see you have the freak with you."

"And I see you have your whore with you." I had longed to say the words for many seasons, and the sight of Jingyi emerging, her hair loose, from the emperor's bedroom made them impossible to hold.

Jingyi looked as though I had stuck her with a knife, but Emperor Lan laughed. "Rich for you to speak of whores as you stand there with your lover and your ill-begotten freak of a son," Lan said. "I was merciful and gave you a way out, Li, but you weren't even smart enough to take it."

Before I could reply he gestured to General Kin. "General, take a full escort and see Lady Matoda arrives safely back at her father's house."

"Captain Bahnu will organise an escort."

"No, General. There are those—" Lan's gaze hung upon me "—who would do harm to the future Empress of Kisia. These are dangerous times and her safety is paramount. You will go yourself."

The usually brusque general hesitated. "In dangerous times, Your Majesty, my place is at your side."

"And as Lady Jingyi will soon be my empress we are as one," the emperor said, turning his scowl from me to his general. "I do not see why my order is so difficult to grasp. You do not like my choice of bride?"

Never had I seen Kin's face redden, but it did so now as he bowed. "Your choice is very fine indeed, Your Majesty, and I assure you that I am not lacking understanding of your order merely concerned for your safety. That is, after all, my job."

"And very good at it you are, but I think even you must agree that six guards are enough to protect me against an unarmed man, an old woman, and a little boy."

Kin nodded the short, sharp nod of a dismissed soldier. "Yes, Your Majesty. When you are ready, Lady Matoda."

"I am ready now, General," she said in her sweet, musical voice, and stopping only to smile upon the emperor she swept from the room as though the rest of us did not exist, her head high and her hands clasped. General Kin followed, but as he stopped to speak a word in Captain Bahnu's ear his eyes lifted to mine and for a moment a different man stood in the general's place, a man whose heart shone through his eyes, whose lips framed words he dared not speak, whose brow furrowed with fear. If only I had some of Nyraek's skill, some of Takehiko's sight, I might have understood without Kin needing to speak. Instead he departed upon the emperor's whim and the door slid closed behind him.

Emperor Lan glared at Nyraek. "That man is worth a hundred of you, Laroth," he said, leaning forward in his chair. "Was humiliating me with a bastard son not enough for you? Have you returned from exile against my orders just to play the hero? What a pathetic end to make."

Nyraek bowed his head. "It was never my intention to humiliate Your Majesty. I—"

"Shivats to your intention," Lan snarled. "I ought to have had you executed, but such things only breed more talk, and you know how I dislike rumours and gossip." His dark eyes snapped to me. "But now you and that bastard boy have made your last breath of trouble."

Takehiko flinched as I put my hands upon his shoulders. "Please, Your Majesty," I said, the pleading words bitter upon my tongue but I had a part to play. "I make no supplication for myself, but you acknowledged Takehiko and have raised him from the cradle as your son, I beg you not to harm him now."

He laughed. "Not harm him? He ought to have been drowned at birth. That's what your people do with freaks, is it not? Why don't we let Lord Laroth make the choice?" The emperor smiled upon his former general. "What is more important, your life or his?"

"His."

Not even a pause for thought. And this was the man whose life I risked to see this through.

"Too easy a question for an honourable man," Lan said. "Let me instead ask which life is more important, this bastard, or your own heir?"

In the silence midnight crept closer. The emperor started to laugh. "You should have chosen your own life, Laroth, it would have been much easier that way. Guards, take the boy."

"No!" *Too soon. Too soon.* "You cannot." Gripping Takehiko's shoulders I pushed him toward the man he had always thought of as father. "Look at him," I said. "This is your son, your boy, named for your grandfather. You cannot do this."

In more than ten years of marriage I had learned that Lan didn't like being told what he could and couldn't do, but his rage at my words far exceeded my expectations. He rose from his chair, red faced and screaming. "How dare you speak such treason to me! I am your husband! Your emperor! Your *god!*"

It looked for one blissful moment as though he would grab Takehiko, but he stepped back with a snarl and jabbed a finger in the boy's face. "Take him away. I want him executed. And both of you will watch him die before your own heads are hacked from their worthless bodies. Get them all out of here."

A guard gripped Takehiko's arm but did not fall, but neither did the boy move except to press a hand to his face as a low keening came from between parted lips. A second guard gripped the hand and yanked it away. "Come, boy," he said. "Let's—"

Takehiko's keening grew louder and the guard went rigid, his eyes popping. And like a stiff board the man fell back, smacking his head upon the leg of a brazier.

"Kill him! Kill him now!" Emperor Lan shouted, backing away. Still holding Takehiko's arm, the first guard drew a dagger only for Nyraek to bring his empty scabbard down upon his head with a mighty crack. Another guard rushed in, sword meeting scabbard as Lord Laroth stood his ground.

The doors slid and the two men posted outside paused a moment to take in the scene while another pushed past me, dagger drawn. I stuck my foot in his gait, catching the toe of his boot. He tripped, but would have regained his balance but for the knife I yanked from my sash. With no time for finesse I stuck it in his back, forcing him down. One cry of pain was bitten short by another as I ripped the knife free and brought it down again. He gripped my foot, tried to roll, but fire filled my veins and I stabbed him again and again.

"Not my son!"

Blood covered my hands, my heart revelling in its stamp as I spun to face the remaining guards. Three lay dead while the other three hung back, hovering before Nyraek. He might have been armed with only an empty scabbard, but he had taught them how to fight, he knew their strengths and their weaknesses, and had too long possessed their loyalty.

"Kill the boy! Now!" the emperor shouted from behind his chair. "Kill them all if you have to."

"I'm sorry, General," Captain Bahnu said, licking dry lips.

"So am I."

He came in, sword swinging. Nyraek caught it on his hacked up scabbard and stepped in only to meet a corpse. A flurry of movement swept through the room owning the vague shape of a man – a gust of wind that stank of wet leaves. And in its wake the meaty thwack of an axe cleaving flesh. Blood spurted. Men fell. And there before us stood Gadjo, breathing heavily and covered in crimson rain.

"Your Majesty," he said, gaze flicking to me over Nyraek's shoulder. "I have come for the boy."

"You cannot have him," Nyraek said.

"This is not your choice, soldier. Step aside."

"Yes, it is. He is my son."

Gadjo's sneer softened as his brows lifted. "Your son?" He glanced at Emperor Lan then, a fleeting look of derision for the god who cowered behind his throne. "Interesting. I'll show you mine if you show me yours."

Nyraek had not retied the bracer upon his arm and thrust it out, a punch into nothing but air. A smile turned Gadjo's lips as he looked upon the birthmark, while in his hand the axe dripped blood onto the matting. In the other hand a knife, stained as red as his fingers. That was the arm he held out in response, no covering to remove as he admitted his aberration to the world. A birthmark shaped like half an arrow glared up at us, so red it might have been scarred upon his skin.

"I have never seen anything like that," Nyraek said.

"If it comes to that, I have never seen one like yours. In another life perhaps this could have been different, but unless Empress Li lets me take your son I am going to have to kill you too."

Curled upon himself, Takehiko rocked back and forth in the middle of the floor, his arms over his head, small hands gripping clumps of his hair. Beside him a body spilled guts like worms.

You need to get up, I thought. *You need to kill the emperor.*

The boy didn't move.

You need to get up. You need to kill the emperor. Then you will be free.

"To what end?" Nyraek said, standing his ground before his son. "Look at him. He is just a child. What is it you need so desperately that you would make such threats to an empress?"

Get up. Kill him.

Gadjo tilted his head. "You mean you don't know?"

"Don't know what?"

He looked to me, laughter in his eyes. "That your son can kill."

Nyraek had been too long a soldier to turn from his enemy, thus sparing me the full force of his hurt, but I could not miss the change in his tone. He licked his lips. "I see."

"Perhaps now you will change your mind and let me remove the burden."

"No."

"Is that your answer, Empress? Because I can go from here and kill your children and be back within a few moments to see if you have changed you mind. I can even bring you their heads if that would be easier."

Movement drew attention to the throne where Emperor Lan had gotten to his feet. "Who in the hells is this man?" he demanded, as though every one of his guards did not now lay dead.

Gadjo didn't turn from me. "My name is Gadjo, Your Majesty," he said. "But perhaps now is not a good time to draw attention to yourself."

"What did you say about the boy?"

"That he can kill, Your Majesty. I imagine that is why he is here at this very moment and why all your guards are dead." He still hadn't turned from me and he smiled then, with a twist that seemed to apologise. "One last play, eh? I can respect that. If I let the boy kill him first, then would you let me take him?"

Emperor Lan dead and the weight of responsibility lifted from my shoulders. And if I did not, he would kill my children. Kill everyone until I agreed. Whatever his unseen abilities, Nyraek was no match for this man.

"Yes."

"No!"

Nyraek jabbed his scabbard into Gadjo's gut and snatched up Captain Bahnu's dropped sword. Its swift

90

upward arc ought to have sliced the servant open, but Gadjo disappeared throwing Nyraek off balance.

"I don't want to kill you," he said, sucking breaths as he reappeared behind him. "It has been many years since I last met another who was... different. But I will if you make me."

"Not if I kill you first."

Gadjo laughed, blurred, and reappeared behind Nyraek again, an arm around his throat tight enough to redden Lord Laroth's features. "That is..." the man said, waving his knife. "Unlikely."

Wind ripped through the room, scattering papers and toppling screens. Unable to keep myself upright against the gale, I hit the matting, and when I hissed out pain, anger crackled with it like lightning. Gadjo slammed into the wall, while in the middle of the floor stood Nyraek, his sword gripped in white knuckles.

"I will not let you take my son," he said, every second word punctuated by a gasp for breath. "If you want him, you will have to fight for him."

Gadjo got to his feet, adjusting his grip upon both axe and dagger. Yet he made no move with either, just stared at Nyraek as though the silence had meaning. Lan, once more behind his throne, watched on as I crawled toward Takehiko. "Mama needs your help," I whispered, setting my hand upon his hunched shoulder. "You'll help me, won't you?"

Silence.

"The emperor is not your father," I went on, barely voicing the words. "Lord Nyraek Laroth is your father and if you do not kill Emperor Lan then your father is going to die."

Still silence.

"I am afraid, Takehiko."

"If you want me dead then come kill me yourself," Emperor Lan said. "Don't send a child to do it for you."

I stood, stung by the jeer. My blade was already stained scarlet, what harm would a little more blood do? Leaving Takehiko I advanced step after deliberate step toward the man I had married all those years ago. Doubt had gnawed at me, but it shed with every step across the bloodied matting.

"You might be able to kill a man taken by surprise, but I was trained too well," Lan said, eyeing my blade.

"And I am always underestimated."

Lan sneered as I approached. "Underestimated? Or—"

He hurled the chair into my path. It caught my leg as I leapt aside, but I didn't fall and spun back crowing with triumph. Crow became cry as a weighted chain smacked into my shoulder. It thrummed on through the air, and fearing its return swing cracking my skull, I flung myself down. But fingers closed amid my hair and an arm threaded around my throat, dragging me up.

"Or overconfident?" Lan said, his heavy breath hot against my ear. "Either way you make a pathetic end, my dear."

His grip strangled all hope of a pithy retort and scattered my thoughts. His arm tightened. Death called. But Takehiko would sense my fear. He would come. He would save me.

But Takehiko did not come.

Clashing metal seeped through the gathering darkness, but I could not turn my head nor even focus upon its source. Blood sprayed upon the matting, its pain cutting the night. Then that pain poured into me, overflowing into agony and I screamed silence. Lan's grip faltered. His breath came in sharp gasps. He let me go, but the pain only grew like fire searing every inch of my flesh.

Lan lurched back, gripping his head. My knife sat upon the matting and I dragged myself through the waves of pain toward it, though each wave threatened to drown me. The room spun, but my fingers found steel. Then with one foot beneath me I lunged. The blade entered his chest first, shuddering off bone. Then again. More ribs. One cracked beneath my barrage, the snap as satisfying as the bloom of blood upon his crimson robe and his guttural cry. He gripped my throat, but his strength was waning. Blood had made my grip slick, but I did not stop, could not get enough of the joy that came with every furious thrust into his chest. His arms. And then his throat. Lan's gaze wavered then, his anger seeping out with his blood, his hands shaking about my neck as he tried to breathe and failed.

I pulled away, dropping the knife. Lan fell with it, first to his knees then rolling on to his side still gasping for air. Joy abandoned me as memory threw up its cruel images. This the man I had married. Whose children I had borne. His laughing eyes, his confident smile, the whisper of sweetness in my ear and the promise of plenty. And there was no goodbye, never could be, because even in that moment I could not forgive.

A roar snatched my attention as Nyraek swung at his opponent, only for Gadjo to disappear and reappear with a breathless laugh. "Just give up," he said. "I won't let you hit me."

Nyraek swung again, pain still sloughing off him to spark along my skin. Anger mingled with it, pushing him on as it pushed me. "Stop!" I shouted, staggering toward them. "It is done! He's dead."

93

Another swing, Nyraek throwing himself at where he knew Gadjo would no longer be. Blood stained his shoulder and his leg, and it dripped down the side of his face, but though Gadjo could have killed him at any time he had not.

Appearing behind Nyraek again, the servant, sagging and gasping for breath, said: "You give me permission to take him?"

"Yes," I said. "Take him. Go. Leave and never return. Don't harm any of my other children."

"Touch him and I will run you through," Nyraek snarled.

"He will kill you if you try," I said, putting blood-stained hands together to plead. "This is the only way. If we don't let him take Takehiko he will kill Yarri and Tanaka and Rikk and still come back for him. And for what? There is no point fighting."

His face set in grim lines. "There is always a point. I will fight until I die because I could not live with myself if I did not. If he wants to take my son then he will have to kill me first."

"Damn your honour! I don't want to kill you," Gadjo said. "I haven't met another freak since my mother was burned for prophesying the death of Empress Li." He turned to me as he spoke, then barked out a harsh laugh. "Fool she is to try and evade what has already been written."

"You're the son of the seer?"

He bowed, sweat flicking from his hair. "At your service, though she was the far more useful one. She is the reason I chose to work for Lord Epontus, because she knew more than she ever told others. She could have told you how you would die. She could have told the emperor that he would die. That his empire would fall. That his palace would burn. That the greatest threat to the throne was much closer than he had ever imagined."

A burst of energy sent me staggering, my mind a swirl of fear and anger and pain. Nyraek thrust his blade for Gadjo's gut and caught his side. The man howled. Blood burst from his tunic, his flesh ripped by the exiting blade. But the killing jab that followed found nothing but air.

When Gadjo reappeared both men staggered, bleeding and broken and unwilling to stop.

"Last chance," Gadjo gasped, clasping his side. "I don't want to do this but I will."

"Then do it."

Somewhere in the scuffle the axe had been thrown down, but Gadjo's short knife was all the better for killing at short range. Of killing the only ally I had left. It unfolded before me. Nyraek would strike. Gadjo would not be where his sword struck and would appear behind him to slice open Lord Laroth's throat. The seer might have said it could not be changed, but I could not lose anymore.

As Nyraek stepped in to strike, I charged at the empty space behind him— and slammed into a wall of flesh. Air burst from my lungs as I fell with Gadjo in a tangle of limbs and sweat and silk. I landed on his legs, stunned and breathless, and before I could roll the bloodstained flat of a blade appeared before me, its point plunged into Gadjo's gut. Pinned to the matting the man thrashed, kicking me off with limbs that moved at the speed of desperation. Only with death did he slow to a natural pace, but though he lifted a shaking hand toward me he had nothing left and in silence he faded, dropping the half-arrow birthmark onto the matting.

Nyraek yanked the sword free.

I did not get to my feet, could not, not yet. My arms trembled and I sat in the spreading blood all too aware of the presence of Nyraek standing beside me.

Only after a few beats of silence passed did he speak. "We have to get out of here before General Kin returns," he said, wide eyes taking in the scene. "By the gods what have we done?"

"What needed to be done," I said, though I hugged my knees to my chest.

He turned those wide eyes upon me, the horror in them stinging. "You wanted this? Why? Because he chose to set you aside for another?"

"No!" I forced myself to my feet then. "I am not so petty. It had to be done to protect Kisia from another war."

Nyraek laughed, a mirthless, bitter laugh. "Protect Kisia from another war? You have made another war a surety. Was this your secret? Is this why Koto died?"

"Lan was planning an alliance with the Curashi. And with the pirates. He was going to attack Chiltae without warning, breaking the treaty and throwing Kisia into a war it could ill-afford. And when our new allies turned on us? What then?"

"And when General Kin returns to find a Chiltaen assassin dead in the emperor's rooms, what then? Do you think Grace Tianto will make peace then?"

He might well have slapped me so harsh were the words, each seeming to end in a laugh he could not shake. I stared down at the still form of Gadjo. "Then we move him. We hide him."

Lord Laroth spread his arms. "Where? Under the sleeping mat? Bodies start to stink after awhile, or didn't you know that? Or are you expecting me to lug a dead body out of here without being seen? Some of the Imperial Guards are still loyal to me, but not that loyal. Their first duty is to the emperor and no one else and it always has been. As it is I will have a hard time getting out." He spat the words, fury lashing from his lips. "Too many people know I was here for me to ever show my face in Mei'lian again. To ever show my face in Kisia! You have made exiles of us all, my dear, and for what? So Prince Yarri can wage the war his father planned."

"We could burn the body."

"Burn it?" He was really laughing now. "Bodies are soggy things, Li, you can't just tip a brazier on it and wait for it to become ash."

"No, but we could tip coals on his face. That way no one would know he was Chiltaen."

The laugh died upon his lips. "You can't be serious."

"I am very serious." I pushed past him and strode to the brazier.

"If you tip that onto the matting it will catch fire and burn the whole place down."

"And why not?"

"Because even if you burn the palace down you still won't be the empress."

I glared at him in silence, hating the grain of truth that made his words sting.

"I should not have said that," he said when the silence grew fat and awkward. Nyraek bowed. "My apologies, but this has not been a good night. Whatever you might have thought of him and whatever his plans, I gave my oath to protect His Majesty and in that I have failed." He shot a glance at Takehiko. The boy had not once moved. "We need to get him out of here. I cannot take him without rousing suspicion. I have to go out the way I came in or even my old friends will not let me go. You need to leave all your things and order a palanquin brought around now before Kin returns. I'll meet you in the city. You know where. Then we can talk properly."

Though covered in drying blood, I nodded. "I will meet you there."

Nyraek let out a deep breath and gripped my arms. "We will get out of Kisia and our son will be safe."

"Yes."

A wry laugh this time, no longer bitter. "Just like we always planned, eh? To run away together to somewhere warm. Somewhere far away."

"I hear there's a place across the Eye Sea where they have no emperors, no kings, no wars. Just herds of horsemen who wander wide grass plains."

"That," he said. "Sounds perfect. Except that we aren't the same people anymore. This can never be forgotten. I ought perhaps to thank you, to hold you, but I cannot be sure what I would pass if I did."

Pain still frayed the air around him.

"I understand. And Nyraek," I added as he went toward the doors. "I am sorry."

The wry smile twisted his lips and he shrugged one shoulder. "Too late." And on those words he went out, pausing in the doorway to look both ways along the passage before disappearing into the darkness.

Takehiko made no sound as I shook him. "We are leaving," I said. "You must run and grab our cloaks and meet me outside the nursery. Can you do that?"

Nothing.

"Juno is already waiting for us." My lie brought him to life in a way that broke my heart, but I forced a smile.

"Good boy. I will be there in a minute, there is something I need to do here first."

Another nod. No words.

"Good. Now run."

He did so, not stopping to look around as Nyraek had done, just dashing out the open doors. I started forward to close them, but there was no time. Any moment more guards could come. Any moment General Kin might return.

A pair of metal tongs hung beneath one of the braziers and I gripped them with the end of my sash. Muttering a prayer to no god in particular, I lifted out the biggest coal and lowered it onto Gadjo's staring eye, hoping the curvature of the socket would keep it from rolling on to the floor. It hissed as I returned to the brazier for another. Though my heart hammered and my hands shook, I got a second pinched in the tongs and returned to the body. The skin around the first was scorching toward black, the stink of burning skin and hair returning me to that cold morning two years ago when his mother, the seer, had started screaming.

My hand shook so much the second coal almost toppled to the floor, but I caught it on the side of the tongs and scooped it into place upon his other eye. Something bubbled and hissed.

I dropped the tongs and turned toward the door only to halt. A man stood in the doorway, not Nyraek, not General Kin, not a guard or a servant or a secretary or even a lord of the court. He was dressed in grey, plain like a commoner except that he wore sturdy leather boots instead of reed sandals. He seemed to take in the room at a blink and a small notch appeared between his brows.

"Who are you?"

"No one," he said, the words more growl than voice. He pointed, and water dripped from the end of his sleeve though it had not been raining. "Is that the emperor?"

"Yes. He... he died."

The knife might always have been in his hand, but he lifted it now and came toward me. "One less."

"Wait! No! I am not the—"

Hot pain cut my flesh. I needed to speak, to plead, but blood came to my mouth instead of words. I scrabbled at the man's arm, his chest, his face, trying to grip anything to stop myself sinking. The room spun until there was no room. Until there was no breath. No sound but the crackle of flames and distant screams.

The smell of charring flesh followed me into the darkness.

You will die before your thirtieth year. Your children will die. The empire will burn.

You don't have to believe in fate. Fate believes in you.

Epilogue

Blood covered the man's hands and rain dripped from his hood, but he heeded neither. Safe beneath his travelling cloak two children slept, one leaning against him upon the horse, the other a baby tucked into a peasant woman's sling. Despite their warmth and the rhythm of their breath, he paid no heed to them either. On through the rain the man rode, eyes upon the night, thoughts somewhere far away. There wasn't much time. He was needed back in Mei'lian, but he was needed here more.

A pinprick of light grew as his horse approached with weary steps, until a priest's wagon appeared from the gloom exactly where he had been told it would be. Something was going right at last – a bitter thought for a bitter cold night.

"Time to wake up," the man said, nudging the child on the horse in front of him.

The boy took his own weight, but did not answer.

Level with the wagon the man got down, taking care not to spill the baby from the sling beneath his cloak. He ought to have looked back to see if anyone followed, ought to have examined the shadows for waiting blades, but he had left such interest in life behind.

The steps of the wagon were slick and the painted door was chipped and worn. He knocked. The whole wagon rocked as someone moved beyond, then the door opened. A man in white stood in the light, a frown marring an otherwise kindly face.

"Brother Jian?"

"Yes?"

The man gestured to the boy on the horse. "I need your help."

Hello readers!

Thank you for picking up 'In Shadows We Fall', I hope you enjoyed it! Please consider taking a moment to share your opinion in a review as nothing changes lives quite like reviews. They help new readers find my work and provide valuable feedback.

If you're interested in hearing about new releases you can sign up to my Quarterly Newsletter at:

www.devinmadson.com

No spam! Ever! Ick. Though I will occasionally run competitions in there, or write little bits of short fiction. Yay for stories!

Or…

Continue the story in The Vengeance Trilogy!

- Devin Madson

CPSIA information can be obtained
at www.ICGtesting.com
Printed in the USA
LVHW090514090420
652781LV00001B/48

9 780995 413344